H. Irving Hancock

The Grammar School Boys in Summer Athletics

H. Irving Hancock

The Grammar School Boys in Summer Athletics

1st Edition | ISBN: 978-3-75236-105-6

Place of Publication: Frankfurt am Main, Germany

Year of Publication: 2020

Outlook Verlag GmbH, Germany.

Reproduction of the original.

The Grammar School Boys in Summer Athletics

By H. Irving Hancock

Chapter I

"There's just one thing that I keep thinking about on a day like this," Dave Darrin sighed contentedly.

"What's that?" Tom Reade wanted to know. "Supper?"

Darrin turned, favoring Reade with a flash of disgust from his large, dark eyes.

"I'm still waiting for the information," insisted Tom after a short pause.

"You may as well wait," retorted Dave. "You wouldn't understand what I feel, anyway. Any fellow who can keep his mind on supper, on a grand June day like this———"

"I imagine that you'll keep your mind on the meal when you reach the table," predicted Tom, grinning.

"That'll be time enough," Dave rejoined. "But I'm not going to profane the woods, on a perfect June day, by thinking of kitchen odors."

"Say, aren't you feeling well?" asked Tom gravely.

"That's just the point, I guess," broke in Dick Prescott, with a light laugh. "Dave is feeling so extremely well and happy———"

"Now, you're shouting," Darrin assented. "But it's no use for poor Reade to ponder over the glories of nature. All he can think of is the region bounded by his belt."

"Glories of nature?" repeated Reade. "If that's what you're talking about, why didn't you announce your subject earlier? Yes, sir; nature is at her greenest best to-day. Just look off through that line of trees, and see how the light breeze moves the tops in that field of young corn, and———"

"Corn?" flared Dave. "Something to eat, of course! Tom, you're hopeless when it comes to the finer things of life. You ought to have been born in a pen, close to a well-filled trough. Corn, indeed!"

"This country would probably be bankrupt if there were no corn crop, and you'd be digging hard for a living, instead of being a lazy schoolboy," retorted Reade, with an indulgent smile. "Let me see; how many hundred million dollars did Old Dut tell us the annual corn crop brings in wealth to this country?"

All of the other boys, save Dave, glanced at Tom, but all shook their heads. Statistics do not mix well in a Grammar School boy's head.

"Oh, well, it was a lot of money, anyway," Tom pursued his subject. "I wouldn't mind having all the money that the American corn crop brings."

"So you could buy the fanciest kinds of food, I suppose?" jeered Dave Darrin.

"Never mind, Darry; if I had a lot of money I'd buy you the biggest and softest mattress I could find, so that you'd have nothing to do but lie off by yourself, look up at the green leaves and dream your summers away. That lying on your back and looking up at the sky is what you call reverie, isn't it?"

"Quit your kidding!" ordered Dave.

"Is it reverie?" asked Harry Hazelton, "or just plain laziness that ails Dave?"

"Laziness, of course," laughed Tom. "Dave, I guess Harry has more sense in naming things than any of us. Yes; that's it! And Dick thought it was merely poetic temperament."

"Temperament? What's that?" grinned Dan Dalzell. "Is that what you get in June by adding up the column of figures in the thermometer?"

To signify his lack of interest in the talk, Darrin rolled over on his side, turning his gaze away from the other boys. In another minute Dave's eyes were closed, his lips open and his breath coming regularly and audibly.

Such was the droning effect of the warm June breezes on this glorious afternoon.

"Give Dave the chorus of 'He Was the Sleepiest Boy,'" whispered Greg to the others. "Put a lot of steam into every line!"

At a sign from young Holmes the drowsy chorus rolled out, punctuated by timely yawns.

Darry rolled over, yawning, too, an easy-going smile on his face.

"Greg," he charged, "I'm certain that you put the crowd up to that outrage. When I summon up energy enough I'm going to thrash you."

"All right," agreed Greg, "I'll take boxing lessons within a year or two, so as to be prepared for you."

"I wish this were to-morrow afternoon," grumbled Harry Hazelton.

"I'm glad it's to-day," sighed Dave easily.

3

"But to-morrow will be Monday, and we can play baseball."

"And just because to-morrow will be Monday," retorted Dave, "Old Dut will expect us to bring in those fifteen examples in insurance."

"We'll be all past that, by afternoon," Dan broke in. "Then, as soon as the bell rings to dismiss school, we'll all pile outside and have a ripping practice on the diamond."

"Yes; we'll have to get a lot of practice," Dick assented. "Otherwise, you know, the North Grammar will just wipe up the field with us Wednesday afternoon."

"The North Grammar!" sniffed Greg scornfully. "Hi Martin's crowd? Huh!"

"Those North Grammar boys have been practising," Dick insisted. "Hard work is what tells in athletics."

"Well, hang it, didn't you keep us running all through the spring?" demanded Dalzell. "Didn't you say that would put us away at the top in Grammar School baseball?"

"It will help us a long way," assented Dick. "Yet it won't do everything. Each of us has to be as nearly perfect as possible in the position that he has to play. That's why we really need a lot more practice than we've had on the real field."

"The worst of it is" suggested Tom, "that we've got all of the best players in the school on our regular nine, and the scrub nine isn't made up of fellows who can really give us any work."

"Don't croak, Dick," begged Dave. "This day is too perfect to have it spoiled by any calamity howling."

Presently Darrin rolled over on his side once more. Greg took a peep, became suspicious, and started to hum:

"He was the Sleepiest Boy."

Smack! came a small sod, with which Dave had slyly provided himself in advance.

"Ugh! Gr-r-r-r!" sputtered young Holmes, leaping to his feet and spitting out the stuff from his mouth. It was mostly the grass side of the sod that had struck his teeth, but a little of the loam had gone in with it.

"Good enough for me, I suppose," grimaced Greg, seating himself once more when he had cleaned his mouth fairly well. Dave, who had turned over to grin at Greg, soon rolled back to his old posture on the grass.

4

Greg, however, was not disposed to let the matter pass as easily as the others imagined. Shortly Holmesy jumped astride of Dave and rolled that youth over on to his back.

"I didn't eat all of the sod," young Holmes announced. "You may have the rest, Darry. How does it taste?"

Dave shut his mouth tightly, but Greg held his nostrils. The instant that Darrin opened his mouth for air Holmes rammed in the piece of sod. Then he jumped up, retreating.

It was now Dave's turn to jump up and work vigorously getting the stuff out of his month.

"Tastes immense, doesn't it, Dave?" called Holmes tantalizingly.

No answer in words came from Darrin, but he suddenly wheeled, charging straight at Greg. Doubtless the latter would have gotten out of the way safely, but that Dick thrust out a foot, tripping Dave as he bounded by.

Darrin came down upon his knees. The hotheaded youth was now very close to being angry in earnest.

"Hold up, Dave!" Prescott advised. "You started it, you know. You will have to show that a joke is just as funny whether it's going or coming."

"That's right, old chap," agreed Dave, halting and beginning to cool. "Greg, come here and shake hands."

"You shake hands with Tom," Holmes retorted suspiciously. "I appoint Tom my substitute, with full powers."

"I'd sooner fight Tom than you," mused Dave, gazing down at Reade, who did not appear to be very much disturbed. "Tom is the fellow who's always bringing his appetite along on the finest days that heaven has sent us."

Dick Prescott lazily drew out his watch and glanced at it. Then he rose, remarking:

"You may stay here and get all the comfort you can out of nature, Dave. But it's half past five and I guess the rest of us will want to be nearer to the source of kitchen odors."

"Whew! If it's any such time as that I'm going to move fast," cried Harry Hazelton, leaping to his feet. "At our house supper is on at six o'clock, and anyone who gets in late has to take what's left."

"Are your folks so poor as that?" laughed Tom.

"Hardly," returned Harry. "But both dad and mother are sticklers for everyone being in his seat on time."

By this time five of the chums had started across the broad, sunny field toward the rather dusty road.

"Coming, Dave?" Dick called, looking back.

"Oh, yes," grunted Darrin. "But I hate to see all of you fellows running as though you didn't know whether you'd ever get another meal."

"I wonder what is Dave's sudden grouch against the eats," Tom mused aloud. "I've seen him at a few meals, and he was always a clever performer."

"Probably Dave has been eating too much for this time of the year, and has a touch of indigestion," Greg laughed.

Darrin overheard the discussion as he came along, but he did not choose to enlighten his friends. However, unintentionally, Greg had touched upon a part of the trouble. Dinner, that Sunday, at the Darrin cottage, had been unusually tempting, and Dave had eaten heavily. For that reason, when he had joined the crowd in the early afternoon, Dave had felt just a bit sluggish. The walk out into the country had roused his digestion a bit, and had left him in just that state where he could contentedly lie on the grass and doze half of the time.

On this bright Sunday all six of our Grammar School boys had attended church and Sunday school as usual. Then, the day being so fine, they had met and gone away on this tramp, which had ended in a "resting match" on the cool grass under the shade of trees.

All of our readers are familiar with these six fine American boys. Our readers were first introduced to Dick & Co., as Prescott and his chums were locally known, in the first volume in this series, "*The Grammar School Boys Of Gridley.*" Therein the reader made the acquaintance of six average American boys of thirteen, and followed them through their sports and adventures—which latter were many and startling indeed.

In the second volume of the series, "*The Grammar School Boys Snowbound,*" the same six were shown at winter sports just before Christmas. The detection, on Main Street, of a trio of Christmas shopping thieves led to a long chain of rousing adventures. Right after Christmas, Dick & Co., securing permission from their parents, went for a few days of forest camping in an old log cabin of which they had been given the use. Another phase of their adventure with the shopping district thieveries turned up in the woods and contributed greatly to the excitement of their experience. While still camping in the old, but weather-proof cabin, the Grammar School boys found themselves snowbound in one of the greatest blizzards that had happened in that section in years. Being hardy boys from much outdoor life, however,

6

Dick & Co., as our readers know, turned hardship into jolly fun, and incidentally made a great discovery in the woods that turned their camping expedition into the local sensation of the hour. The reader also remembers how some of the poorer specimens of High School boys and a few local young "toughs," under the leadership of Fred Ripley and Bert Dodge, tried to drive them from their forest camp.

In the third volume of the series, *"The Grammar School Boys In The Woods,"* Dick Prescott and his chums, each now fourteen years of age, found the most startling of all the exciting happenings that had been crowded into their short lives. How they came upon two dangerous, tattered specimens of humanity in the woods, how these two contrived to make Dick and Greg take unwilling part in an attempt to rob one of the local banks, the mystery of the haunted schoolhouse, and a host of other lively incidents—-all these are so familiar to the reader of these volumes as to need no repetition. And Dick & Co., through the series of exciting adventures they had encountered, had become the best-known boys in and around the little city of Gridley. Being leaders of other boys, they had naturally made some enemies, but that is to be expected in the case of all who are born to lead, or who fit themselves for leadership.

And now, on this glorious June Sunday afternoon, we find our schoolboy friends enjoying the sacred day quietly, yet looking forward to the opening of the contests on the diamond between the three local Grammar Schools, the North, Central, and South Grammars.

The road they had chosen on this Sunday afternoon was one over which they had seldom traveled. It was not the road to Norton's Woods, to the great forest, nor yet the one that went by the "haunted schoolhouse." It was in a wholly different direction from Gridley.

"It's a long way home, this," complained Tom Reade, as the boys plodded along the dusty highway. "And I'm hungry."

"Hungry?" snorted Darrin. "Of course you are. You fellows sang a verse to me a while ago. Tom, how do you and your fellow-porkers like this lay?"

Taking a deep breath, Dave started to sing a travesty, to the air of "America."

"My stomach, 'tis of thee, Sweet gland of gluttony, To thee I sing! Gland—-"

"Stop it," ordered Tom threateningly, as he advanced upon Darrin.

"Stings, does it?" inquired Dave sarcastically.

"Yes, it does," Reade retorted bluntly. "To my mind 'America' is as sacred as any hymn ever written, and I won't hear it guyed! That's no decent occupation for an American boy."

"That's right," nodded Greg Holmes.

"Well, I won't yield to any of you in being American to the backbone," Dave retorted hotly.

"Prove it," said Tom more quietly.

"I'll prove it by my whole life, if need be," Darrin went on warmly. "Tom Reade, I'll be glad to meet you when we're sixty years old, talk it all over and see who has been the better American through life!"

"Great!" laughed Dick Prescott approvingly. "That'll be a fine time to settle the question. And that time is——let me see——forty-six years away."

The other boys were grinning now, and Dave and Tom, catching the spirit of the thing, laughed good-humoredly.

"But this does seem a mighty long way home," Dan complained.

"I can show you fellows a shorter way, if you want it," Prescott proposed.

"We all live on Missouri Avenue. Show us," begged Hazelton.

"It's through the woods," Dick continued. "I warn you that you'll find some of it rough going."

"Then I don't know about it," Greg replied with fine irony. "We fellows are not very well used to the woods."

"It's twenty minutes of six," declared Dan, glancing at his watch. "Some of us are in danger of eating nothing but cold potatoes tonight if we don't get over the ground faster. Find the short cut, Dick."

"It starts down here, just a little way," Prescott answered. "I'll turn in when we come to the right place."

Dick and Darrin were now walking side by side in advance. Right behind them came Greg and Dan, while Tom and Harry, paired, brought up the rear.

"In this way," called Dick, turning sharply to the left and going in under an archway of trees. It was over velvety grass that he led his chums at first. After something like an eighth of a mile the Grammar School boys came to deeper woods, where they had to thrust branches aside in making their way through the tangle.

"My Sunday suit will look like a hand-me-down by the time I get home," muttered Greg Holmes.

"It does now," Dave called back to him consolingly.

"We suspected that Darry's grouch was due to dyspepsia," laughed Holmes.

"Now I am sure of it. David, little giant, take my advice——fast to-night."

"I will, if the rest of you fellows will," challenged Darrin quickly.

"The truth is out," Tom burst out laughing. "Darry, by that slip of the tongue you admitted that you've been eating too much and that you're all out of sorts."

Dave did not deny. He merely snorted, from which sign of defiance his chums could gain no information.

They had gone another quarter of a mile through the woods when Dick, now alone in the lead, suddenly halted, holding up one hand as a signal to halt, while he rested the fingers of his other hand over his lips as a command for silence.

"What is it?" whispered Darrin, stepping close.

"Fred Ripley, Bert Dodge and some of their fellows," Dick whispered, at the same time pointing through the leaves.

"Well, we don't have to halt, just because they're around," retorted Darrin, snorting. "If they try to pick any trouble with us we can give 'em as good as they send. We've done it once or twice already."

"But we don't want to go to fighting on Sunday, if there's any way to avoid it," young Prescott urged, at which four of his chums nodded their heads approvingly.

"I'm not looking for any fight, either," muttered Dave. "Yet it goes against the grain to halt just in order to let that gang slip by without seeing us."

"There are five of us against your single vote, Darry," Dick reminded him. "Let us have our way."

"Well, we don't need to skulk, do we?" queried Dave.

"Oh, no," Dick assured him. "All we will do is to keep quiet and not bring on a fight with that tough lot."

"Huh!" muttered Darrin, as though he could not see the difference between that and skulking.

Presently, after holding a hand behind him to signal silence and stealth, Prescott started on in the lead. He wanted, if possible, to see just where Ripley, Dodge and their crowd went, so that the Grammar School boys would not run too suddenly into them. The "Co." trailed on in Indian file behind their leader.

Finally Dick halted again, his chums crowding on his heels. They looked out into a clearing beyond. There, amid trees, stood a small three-room house, looking still quite new in its trim paint, though the building had stood there idle for some five years. At one time the city had planned a new reservoir site on a hill just above, and this little cottage had been intended for the reservoir tender. Then a better site for the reservoir had been found, and, to date, the cottage had not been removed.

"Ripley and his crew went around that cottage to the door side," Dick whispered.

"Are they in the cottage?" Dave demanded.

"I don't know. They went around to the other side. Let's wait and see if we can guess what's up."

So, forgetful of their suppers for the time being, Dick & Co. waited, screened by the bushes.

"There's smoke coming up out of the chimney," whispered Tom Reade.

"Yes," nodded Dick. "I had just noticed that. I'm wondering what it can mean. No one has any right to break into the cottage."

"Fred Ripley and Bert Dodge, because they have a lawyer and a bank officer for fathers, don't feel that they need any rights when they want to do a thing," muttered Darrin resent fully.

It was impossible to see what might be going on inside the cottage, for the simple reason that all of the windows were shuttered tightly.

"Let's go ahead," begged Dave, after a few more moments spent in idle watching. "I want to know why that crowd has broken into the cottage."

Truth to tell, even the leader of Dick & Co., usually very discreet, felt himself a victim of curiosity.

"Shall we try to find out the secret, fellows?" Prescott inquired.

"That's just what we ought to do," responded Greg. "Especially as Ripley and Dodge have always been so mean to us."

Dick went forward, with his best imitation of the way he imagined an Indian scout would approach a strange house. Greg and Dan were at his heels, while Dave and Harry went around the other side of the cottage, Tom remaining well to the rear to watch.

Some low, vague sounds came from within the cottage. These were not such noises as scurrying rats would make, so the boys were quick to conclude that human beings were moving inside.

But what could possibly be going on? The noises that the Grammar School boys heard were hard to classify.

At last Dick and Dave met before the door of the little cottage. Nor were they much surprised at finding that the door of the cottage stood perhaps a half an inch ajar.

This, however, did not furnish light enough to give a glimpse of what was happening inside.

"Two or three of us may as well slip inside, eh?" whispered Dave to Dick.

"Wait! Listen!" counseled Prescott. "We don't want to please that crowd by stepping right into a trap. And I've an idea that by this time they must know that we're around here."

"If they knew, they'd be out here making faces at us," retorted Darrin wisely.

"And ordering us to get off the earth," supplemented Greg, in a whisper.

"Listen," whispered Dick. "Perhaps we can guess what they're doing."

"I can guess what they're doing," murmured Reade, who had now moved around to the front with his chums. "I've been watching the smoke of that fire come up through the chimney. Humph! I don't believe Rip and Dodge are doing anything worse than a little camping. There must be a stove in there, and they're cooking some supper——playing at camping out."

"I don't smell anything cooking in there," rejoined Dick with a shake of his head. "We can't hear anything sizzling over the fire, either."

"Then what——-" began Harry curiously.

Bang! interrupted a crashing explosion inside the building. Boom! Then the door flew wide open, followed by a single great belching of white smoke.

Through the center of this cloud was hurled a human figure. A man struck the ground and lay there, senseless or lifeless, a pool of blood quickly forming on the ground beside him.

Chapter II

For the first few seconds the Grammar School boys stood as if chained to the ground, their eyes staring with alarm and horror.

They stared at the man, apparently of middle age, who lay there, and they beheld the blood.

What on earth could have happened?

Boom! It was a lesser explosion that now sounded inside, yet it was enough to galvanize the boys into action.

"Come on!" cried Tom Reade, setting off in the lead. "We don't know nor care what's in there!"

"The house may blow up next," added Greg, following him.

All the members of Dick & Co. were now in full retreat. They were courageous lads, but, with the immediate landscape in seeming danger of blowing up, getting away was the wisest possible course.

"Say, what do you make of that?" demanded Greg breathlessly, when the Grammar School boys had halted, well out of sight of the cottage and down in the woods.

"Bang!" replied Tom dryly. "That's all I heard."

"And blood," almost chattered Hazelton.

"But what it means is a big puzzle," Dick added. "If Rip and his crowd are or were in the cottage, they would hardly explode anything purposely and perhaps kill a man. That man appeared to be dead——he must be dead. Rip and Dodge are mean fellows, but they're hardly up to killing people."

"There was an explosion," remarked Tom judicially, though his voice was still husky. "Now, while I don't know everything, I believe there always has to be an explosive in order to bring about an explosion. Am I right?"

"You stand on ground that no one can dispute," nodded Dick. "But how did the explosive come to be in a building that belongs to the water company, and which is supposed not to have been occupied in some years?"

"What was the man doing in there, for that matter?" demanded Tom.

"He wasn't very well dressed," observed Harry.

"Yet he didn't look like a tramp," Dave put in.

"But the man himself, and the fact that he's hurt or dead, are our two first points to consider," spoke Dick quickly. "If he's hurt we are bound to bring him help. If he's dead, we'll have to notify—-some one."

"I'd like to go back there and have a look at him," quoth Tom, "but the biggest explosion of all may come out of that cottage at any moment now."

"Yet the facts are that another explosion hasn't come, and that the man ought to have help, as a matter of common decency," Dick urged.

"I'll run to the nearest house where people are living," suggested Tom, pulling off his jacket and making ready for a run.

"What are you going to tell the folks?" Prescott queried. "That the poor fellow is living or dead? I'm going back to find out which."

"We'll all go," offered Dave.

"But what happened to Rip and his mean crew?" asked Hazelton.

"We haven't seen any signs that they were in the cottage at all," Dick responded. "If they were, as none of them came out, they must be badly hurt —-perhaps worse."

As a matter of fact, Ripley and his party had not gone into the cottage, but had continued directly towards their homes.

That grisly thought gave all the boys a shudder as they plodded up the slope, between the bushes and thence stepped into the clearing.

"Talk about dreaming!" muttered Dick, halting abruptly and staring hard at the ground around the cottage.

In the first place, the cottage door was closed. There was no smoke now coming out of the chimney, and all looked peaceful and deserted, save for the presence of the Grammar School intruders. There was no injured man lying on the ground.

"Crackey!" gasped Greg. "Yet we didn't all dream together, did we?"

"Certainly not," muttered Dick, again starting forward. The others followed him.

"This is where we saw the man fall, isn't it?" asked Dick.

"Yes," nodded Greg.

"But there was blood on the ground then," urged Dave. "I don't see any now."

"It must have been goblin blood, then," laughed Tom rather unsteadily, for this mystery began to look unearthly.

"Hold on," hinted Dick. "Doesn't it look as though fresh earth had been sprinkled here?"

"Of course it does," nodded Harry. "And the earth has soaked up the blood."

"I don't see any soaked-up blood," objected Greg.

"No; because it's so well covered and soaked up," argued Hazelton. "But wait until I find a stick, and we'll stir up that dirt. Then we'll find the red stuff mixed to a sort of mud, and——"

"Come along out of this, you ghoul!" uttered Tom almost wrathfully, as he seized his friend by the arm.

"We'll go to the door," Dick suggested. "Perhaps we can get inside. At any rate, we can find out whether there is any one inside who wants help."

Dick put his hand on the doorknob, giving it a turn and a hard push.

"Door's locked tightly now," he announced.

"And it takes human hands to lock a door," Reade observed sagely.

"Is there anyone inside who needs any help?" Prescott called loudly.

All was silent inside. Then Dick played a tattoo on the locked door with his fists. Still no sound from inside.

"All together, now," urged Dick. "Any——one——want——help?" bawled six lusty young voices in unison.

"There is only one voice that answers," continued Dick, after a pause, as he turned to the others. "That's the silent voice of good sense."

"What does it say, then," challenged Dave.

"That we've done about all we can do here," Dick replied. "All we know is that a man seemed to have been hurt here. If he was, he was able to take himself away, and to conceal the signs of his hurt before going. Therefore we've no further excuse for meddling around here that I can see."

"Let's get along then," Tom urged. "And——whew! It's after half past six!"

"You'd better run, then," jeered Dave. "Your stomach won't allow any more fooling!"

"Now, what ought I to say to a crank like Darry?" demanded Reade, turning to Prescott.

"You'd better overwhelm him, by saying what the man on the clubhouse steps

14

said," urged Dick.

"And what was that?" asked Tom eagerly.

"We-ell," hesitated Dick, "I believe that's still a secret."

The Grammar School boys were now walking rapidly through the woods, but at mention of the clubhouse topic all had gathered close to their young leader.

"Aren't you going to tell us now?" demanded Greg.

"I'm afraid not right away," responded Prescott slowly.

"See here, Dickins," growled Dave Darrin, "for months you've been stringing us about what the man on the clubhouse steps said. Time and again you've sprung that on us, and you've never given us the slightest satisfaction. Now, you'd either better tell us, or shut up about the man on the clubhouse steps."

"All right," sighed Dick. "I'll———-"

"Well?" insisted five boys in the same breath.

"I reckon I'll shut up," Dick rejoined.

"Say, somebody ought to hit Dickins!" grunted Reade.

"That's right," grinned Dan. "Well—-let Tom do it."

Dick continued to smile mysteriously. He enjoyed this good-natured teasing of his chums.

"What are we going to tell folks about what we saw at the cottage?" queried Dan after another five minutes of trudging.

"If we tell anything at all," suggested Prescott, "I'll tell you how we can win a prize."

"How?" demanded Tom innocently. "By telling the truth," Dick smiled. Soon after the Grammar School boys came out on the road.

"See that group 'way ahead there?" asked Tom, pointing down the road.

"Yes," nodded Dick. "That's Rip's crowd, so we know they didn't get hurt."

"Then the only one who did get hurt," Tom added, "was the man who was very soon able to take mighty good care of himself."

"So we don't need to bother about the matter any more," Greg hinted. "And, gracious! I hope mother has saved some supper for me."

"It'll be a cold hand-out for me," groaned Hazelton.

The Grammar School boys were soon on Main Street now. They hurried along, as they had not yet come to the point of parting.

"Look at that crowd down the street," called Dave. "There's some excitement in the wind."

"I'm not nosey," observed Tom.

"No," scoffed Darrin; "you're too hungry."

"I'm going to see what the excitement is about, anyway," muttered Hazelton, starting forward off a run.

One by one the other boys yielded to curiosity and started at a jog-trot for the corner where the crowd was gathered.

"No; the poor fellow isn't crazy in the ordinary sense of the word," Dick heard a tall man, finely dressed in black, say to some of the bystanders. "He's harmless enough, and his mind isn't permanently astray, if only he can have prompt and good care. But he's inclined to get away by himself and ponder over his inventions. If he leads a too solitary life long enough he may be past the possibility of a cure one of these days. That is why Colonel Garwood is so anxious to find his son, and offers such a handsome reward for information."

"Some one missing?" asked Dick in a low voice.

"Yes," nodded a man in the crowd. "A crazy inventor is lost, or he's loose, at any rate, and his old father is trying to find him. There is a reward of twenty-five hundred dollars for the lucky fellow who finds this inventor with the monkey wrenches in his brain."

"What does the man look like?" asked Dick.

The tall man in black overheard the question and wheeled quickly.

"Amos Garwood is the missing man," said the tall man. "He is forty-seven years of age, about five feet eight in height, slightly stooped, very pallid and with cheeks slightly sunken. When last seen Amos Garwood was rather poorly dressed. He has just escaped from a sanitarium, and the only person who has seen him since reports that he looked 'hunted' and anxious, and that his cheeks were considerably sunken. Garwood has dark hair, slightly gray at the temples. He probably weighs about———-"

"Pardon me, sir," Dick interposed. "What kind of beard does the missing man wear?"

"Dick Prescott has found him," laughed one man in the crowd.

"Garwood has no beard at all, save for what there may be for three or four days' lack of shaving," quickly replied the tall man.

"Where is the missing man, Dick?" laughed another man in the crowd.

"Yes; Dick has found him," called another.

"I rather think so," Dick nodded. "At least, I believe our crowd has seen Garwood very lately."

Prescott's evident confidence aroused instant curiosity.

"Where?" demanded a dozen voices quickly.

"I wish you young men wouldn't answer, but just come with me," spoke the tall man quickly. "If your information proves correct, and we find the missing man, the reward will be yours."

Dick turned to nod to his companions, as the tall man in black turned to lead the way. Their guide, after making sure that Prescott was at his side, walked rapidly down the street a few doors, halting before the street door of one of the office buildings.

"Come upstairs and tell Lawyer Ripley whatever you know," requested the tall man.

"I don't believe you'll find him in Sundays," replied Dick.

"We shall to-day," responded their guide confidently. "Mr. Ripley is helping us in this search."

This, then, looked like proof that the Garwood family was well-to-do, for Lawyer Ripley seldom worked for small fees.

Running ahead, the tall man threw open the door of the lawyer's office.

"Mr. Ripley," he called, "here are some boys who think they have seen Amos Garwood. Probably these youngsters are half dreaming, yet they may have some information of value."

"I know these boys," nodded the lawyer, looking up, "and they are dependable. They are good, bright boys. Prescott, come forward and tell me just what you know, or think you know."

"First of all, sir," urged Dick, "let me give the best description I can of the man we've seen."

"A good idea," nodded Mr. Ripley. "Go ahead."

Nor had young Prescott been engaged very long in his task of description before the tall man broke in excitedly:

"That's our man, beyond a question! Where did you see him? When?"

Dick hastily recounted the strange happenings at the supposedly untenanted cottage of the old water-works project.

"We must get there without delay," called the tall man to two other men who, so far, had kept in the background in the lawyer's office, but who had been deeply interested hearers. "One of you boys must go up there with us. How far is it from here?"

"Come through into my rear office," suggested Mr. Ripley, "and I can show you the spot from a window. Come along, Prescott, and tell me if I'm right. Hello! There seems to be some trouble up that way," added Mr. Ripley, as he reached one of the windows at the rear.

"There's a fire up there under the hill," cried Dick Prescott, as he pressed forward to another window. "Mr. Ripley, from the location of the smoke, I should say that the cottage itself is afire!"

"And I believe you're right," agreed the lawyer.

"Poor Amos!" groaned the tall man. "The poor fellow may have set fire to the place to destroy himself! Ripley, I can't wait here, inactive, another second. We must start! Can I get a cab here?"

"I think I can get an automobile for you inside of five minutes," replied the lawyer, hurriedly leading the way to the front office.

"Five minutes?" groaned the stranger. "Why not wait a year?"

"An automobile will save you much more than five minutes' time on the way," returned the lawyer, snatching up his desk telephone. "Central, give me 163-J in a hurry!"

A few minutes later the automobile was at the door. The tall stranger and two other men who had been in the lawyer's office were now on the sidewalk.

"Crowd on all the speed you can, my man," appealed the tall stranger. "If you get into any trouble with the authorities I'll pay all the fines you incur. This is a matter of life and death."

The speaker and his two men crowded into the car.

"You come, too," called the tall one to Dick.

"Is there room for one other boy?" asked Dick.

"Yes; we can squeeze him in."

"Want to come, Dave?" Dick inquired.

Darrin was by his chum's side in an instant.

"Let out the speed!" ordered the tall man. "Prescott will tell you where to go."

Four members of Dick & Co. had been worrying about their suppers, but now not one of them but would have waited indefinitely for a chance to go on that one especial auto trip.

"Greg, tell my folks where I've gone, and why," Dick shouted back.

Then—-whizz! The automobile was down the street and around a corner before anyone could say "Jack Robinson!"

Chapter III

The automobile party arrived just in time to see the blazing roof of the little cottage crash inward, sending up a shower of sparks against the sky of the dying day.

"I hope Amos wasn't inside, hurt and helpless!" gulped the tall stranger, leaping outside. "But why hasn't the fire department been out here?"

"The Gridley fire department doesn't respond outside of city limits, except on request and by permission of the mayor, sir," Prescott answered.

"I'll drive down and telephone any message for you," offered the chauffeur, who had left his ear behind and had traveled on foot up to the cottage.

"Firemen would be of little use now," replied the man in charge of the party. "We can do nothing until the blazing embers cool, which won't be for hours yet. Still, We might go as close to the blaze as possible, and see if there are any signs of a human body in the embers."

While this was being done darkness came down over the summer day. There was plenty of light, however, around the destroyed cottage.

For some time the searchers explored as well as the heat of the glowing embers would permit.

"I am satisfied," said the tall man at last, "that no human being was consumed in this fire. If so, we would certainly see some evidences of remains. Still, these ashes, when cool, must be searched."

"You don't need me any more, do you, sir?" asked Dick.

"Is it near your bedtime yet?" smiled the stranger.

"I haven't had my supper yet," Prescott smiled. "Neither has Darrin."

"Bless me! What a brute I am to forget a boy's stomach!" cried the tall one. "Here," taking a banknote from his pocket, "I will have the chauffeur drive you back to town and then return for us. Take this money and get the best supper you can for two, at the best restaurant in Gridley."

"Thank you, sir," replied Dick, shrinking back; "our parents wouldn't allow us to do that."

"Are your parents any easier on such questions?" smiled the stranger, turning to Darrin.

"Not a bit, sir, thank you," Dave responded.

"I may at least pay you something for your kindness and trouble in coming out here with me," urged the stranger, still offering the cash.

But both boys shook their heads, declining with thanks. Neither had been reared to accept money for doing a human kindness.

"If you don't need us any more," Dick went on, "we'll just find the road and jog back."

"If you won't accept anything else," retorted the tall man, "you will at least allow me to send you back in the auto. And you will also accept the thanks of John Winthrop, and of Colonel Garwood, whom I represent."

Both boys protested, with thanks, that they were able to get home on their own feet. Mr. Winthrop, however, insisted on their going in the car. Truth to tell, both youngsters had used their feet so much that day that they did not object to being taken home.

"I hope you will find your man, sir, and alive," Dick called, as he and Dave were leaving.

"I believe that we shall," replied Mr. Winthrop. "Yet it will be by beginning the search from this point."

The chauffeur drove them home in good time, for he was under orders to report back to Mr. Winthrop as speedily as possible.

Neither Dick nor Dave had any trouble in getting a late supper served at home.

"You've brought home a good tale, as you often do, to pay your mother for her extra trouble," laughed Mr. Prescott.

"I hope that poor, half-witted fellow didn't destroy himself in his own fire," murmured Dick, as he fell to at the meal.

By morning the people of Gridley knew that the ruins of the abandoned water-works cottage had been explored, and that the remains of Amos Garwood had not been found there.

But an editorial in the "Blade" suggested that the cottage was not very likely to have taken fire unless the blaze had been started by Garwood. While the latter was declared not to be dangerous, the "Blade" hinted that his malady might suddenly have taken a dangerous turn.

"The good people of this section will feel much easier," concluded the editor, "when they know that Garwood has been found and returned to the sanitarium that awaits him. A cash reward of twenty-five hundred dollars should be incentive enough to set many people to the task of finding the unfortunate man."

Yet, for Dick & Co., the adventure of the afternoon before dropped very quickly into the background. Here was Monday; on Wednesday the boys of the Central Grammar must meet the boys of the North Grammar on the diamond. Then the first of a series of baseball games was to be played for the local Grammar School championship. The South Grammar would also enter a nine.

Intense rivalry prevailed between the schools. The fact that the respective nines were made up almost wholly of boys who were soon to be graduated from the Grammar Schools did not in any sense lessen the rivalry. Each young player was proud of his own school and anxious to capture the laurels.

"Are you going to win Wednesday's game from the North Grammar, Dick?" asked Len spencer, when that reporter met Prescott on Main Street at noon on Monday.

"Of course we are," Dick replied instantly.

"You seem very positive about it," quizzedLen.

"That's the only way to go into athletics," claimed Dick. "A team must enter with the determination and the knowledge that it is going to win. Then there's little left to do but to walk home with the victory."

"But Hi Martin was telling me, this morning, that Central hasn't a ghost of a show against North," pursued Len.

"Hi Martin will know better, day after tomorrow, won't he, Dave?" queried Dick, appealing to Darrin, who had just come along.

"He surely will," nodded Dave.

"By the way," asked Len, "have you seen any of the new uniforms of the North Grammar?"

"No," Dick admitted, his face falling a trifle. "I understand that Martin's fellows are going to wear pretty dandy uniforms, though."

"They are," Len nodded. "I've had a look at the uniform."

"Well, North Grammar is attended by a lot of sons of pretty well-to-do men," Dave put in. "Our boys don't come from as wealthy families, so we have to be content with less of the showy things in life."

22

"What are your uniforms going to be like?" inquired Len Spencer.

"We haven't any," Dick replied promptly.

"No uniforms at all?" demanded the "Blade" reporter.

"None at all," Dick continued. "Neither have the South Grammar boys. In the glories of uniform the North Grammar nine will be all in a class by itself."

"It's too bad," muttered Len.

"No, it isn't," Prescott retorted. "We fellows from Central are going to show that uniforms don't necessarily make players. We don't mind—-that is, not very much—-the absence of uniforms."

"We'll try to show that we have something uniform about our team play, and let it go at that," said Dave cheerily. "Come along, Dick, or we'll be late at school."

Away the pair raced. Lessons went about as usual that afternoon with Old Dut's class, which was surprising, as nearly every boy in the room had his mind much on baseball.

Captain Dick Prescott, of the Central Grammar nine, had called practice for that afternoon, from half past four to six o'clock.

At recess, that afternoon, a pleasant, somewhat rotund-looking man was seen engaged in conversation with Old Dut in a corner of the schoolyard. At the close of the afternoon session that same man stepped into the schoolroom, accepting the principal's offer of a chair on the platform.

"Attention!" called Old Dut, striking the bell. "I am glad to be able to state that no pupil has incurred the penalty of remaining after school to-day. However, I am going to ask the members of the Central Grammar baseball nine and their substitutes to remain for a few minutes. I pledge myself not to interfere with the scheduled practice," continued the principal dryly. "All other pupils will file out promptly, and not loiter in coatrooms or corridors."

Within two minutes the place had been cleared of all but Dick's baseball squad.

"I now wish, young gentlemen," began Old Dut, "to introduce to you Mr. Edson Brown, who is interested in baseball, and who has a slight favor that he wishes to ask of you."

"It's very simple," declared Mr. Brown, rising and stepping down from the platform. "I have been greatly interested in baseball for a number of years. Among other things I have a considerable collection of figures concerning school teams, their sizes and weights, I would like, with your permission, young gentlemen, to take a few measurements. I won't detain you more than a few moments."

"Do you want a suggestion, sir?" asked Tom Reade.

"Of course," nodded Mr. Brown, smilingly.

"Then the real crowd that you ought to measure are the fellows of the North Grammar nine. You'd get a fine lot of chest measurements there, I can promise you."

"Why?" asked Mr. Brown. "Are the North Grammar boys better developed physically?"

"I can't say about that," Reade replied seriously, "but they're the only Grammar School fellows in Gridley that have baseball uniforms, and I understand that they're the chestiest lot of young fellows that any one ever saw."

"I'll consider the North Grammar boys later, then," nodded Mr. Brown, smiling. "Now, will each young man oblige me by removing his coat and vest and stepping forward for the measurements that I want to take?"

In a notebook Mr. Brown jotted down the measurements that he made. There being five substitute players, there were fourteen boys in all whose measurements he recorded.

"That is all," nodded Mr. Brown finally, snapping his notebook and tucking it away in a pocket. "I am deeply indebted to all of you young men.

"And now I beg to add," said Old Dut, "that, as all of you youngsters are in a hurry, there will be no criticism if you see fit to race through the corridors."

Out on the field, just before half past four, Captain Dick Prescott lined up his squad of fourteen, himself included, and quickly added four more to the number, thus organizing two nines.

"Now, play ball," he called.

"Do it in a hurry," supplemented Tom Reade.

"Speed is all right," Dick retorted. "But we want to play with care, even more than with speed. The scrub nine will go to bat."

Dick himself ran quickly out to the pitcher's box, twirling his ball impatiently. A High School boy had been secured for umpire, and all was in readiness.

Of course the school nine won over the scrub. Never mind the score, which looked badly for the scrub. Dick was satisfied that his nine was doing the best that was in it.

Tuesday afternoon there was more practice, though Captain Dick did not allow it to continue too long.

"Now, don't take a single chance with yourselves," called Prescott, in dismissing the squad on the field near the schoolhouse. "Don't any one of you get a sore toe or strain a 'wing' before to-morrow afternoon. Fellows, I believe that we are going to be able to put it all over the North Grammar to-morrow afternoon. But we can't do it unless we are all in the best of shape. Be careful at table. Don't any one of you overeat between now and the game. And all get into bed early to-night and have a long sleep."

"I put every young man in this room on honor for to-day," stated Old Dut, facing his class, the next morning. "No matter what the disorder or breach of discipline, no boy will be kept in after school this afternoon, for I know that every one of you, whether player or 'booster,' wants to be at the inter-school ball game this afternoon. So remember, young men, that you are all on your honor to-day. Prove yourselves worthy of it."

Never had discipline been better preserved in the eighth grade classroom than during that day.

Soon after four o'clock scores of Gridley schoolboys had found their way to the big vacant field not far from the Central Grammar, the owner of which permitted its use freely by schoolboy athletes.

The principal of the South Grammar, too, was there, flanked by rough-and-tumble Ted Teall and the South's baseball delegation. Captain Ted had to play the Centrals on Saturday, and he wanted to view their style. Though North Grammar was well represented, the principal of the school did not appear, being "detained by pressure of important duties."

"Old Dut will know enough to be here," remarked one of the Central boys proudly. "Nothing but disaster could keep him from showing interest in our work."

Cheering was started by a big group of North Grammar boys. A stage had just been sighted, and this bore the North Grammar's diamond champions. A few moments later the stage drew up at the edge of the field, and Hi Martin and his fellows piled out, each proudly resplendent in showy uniform of red and white, with red caps and stockings. The North Grammar boys were dandies, and they appeared to want, everyone to realize the fact. They formed at the roadside and marched on to the field in step.

"Halt!" commanded Captain Hi Martin. Then he looked around curiously.

"If the Centrals are here yet, why don't they come out of the crowd and receive us?" inquired Martin rather pompously. His insinuation that Dick's fellows might be mixed with the crowd was a slur on the Central boys not possessing uniforms.

"Our fellows are not here yet, but they will be soon, you bet," called back a Central boy. "It's only twenty minutes past four."

"Spread out, men, and practice," directed Hi Martin.

"Yah! yah!" jeered a Central boy. "Get all the practice you can—-you'll need it."

"These ragamuffins are pretty full of brag," observed Hi scornfully to one of his lieutenants.

"They're just the kind of fellows that always do brag," returned the player addressed. "Their brag will all be gone within a half an hour. You'll see."

"Yes," agreed Hi thoughtfully. "If we can't trim this crowd to-day, then they're some wonders at ball. They don't have any idea how long we've been training in order to give them this trimming."

Some of Hi's players had already spread out over the field, and were doing some rapid passing. Certainly Hi's fielders promised well, from the little glimpse of their skill that was now had.

Then one of their best batsmen took up the willow, driving a few long, swift fielders.

"This will get the Centrals nervous before they start, if they see any of our work," laughed one of Hi's players.

Truth to tell, the North Grammar boys did show some pretty work. Ted Teall looked on approvingly.

"Prescott has met his match to-day," remarked Ted to a friend.

"These Norths will bother you, too, won't they, Ted?"

"Us? No; not a bit. We can play all around the Norths. But Central will have to take third place when the series is done."

"The Centrals haven't got rattled and skulked, have they?" called Hi Martin at last.

A disdainful yell came back from the assembled Central boys.

"Then some one hurry over and tell 'em that it's time to hustle on to the field and take their medicine," urged Hi. "We don't want to have the game called for darkness before we're half through."

26

"The Centrals will be here on time," called back one of Old Dut's boys. "Don't you worry any about them. Dick Prescott is holding the watch over our crowd."

"It's four twenty-seven," announced Hi, consulting his gold watch.

"Four twenty-five and a half," corrected a Central boy.

"Go get your watch fixed," retorted Hi scornfully. "And some one else run and see if he can find out where the Centrals are hiding."

"Here they come!" yelled one excited Central boy. "Whoopee! They will answer for themselves!"

In an instant the Central cheering became tumultuous. Even Ted Teall rubbed his eyes and gasped.

For the Central Grammar School squad was marching toward the field, having just left the schoolhouse. At the head of all, chin well up, marched Old Dut. Back of him, two and two, marched Dick Prescott and his players. What marvel had been worked? For the Central boys wore uniforms that made Hi Martin's fellows look like so many gaudy figures on a cheap poster!

Chapter IV

"Great Scott!" gasped Hi Martin, in sheer dismay, his gaze fixed on the approaching Centrals.

"Where in the mischief did they get those uniforms?" demanded Tom Percival, of the North Grammars, his mouth agape.

"Well, they have 'em, anyway," added Bill Rodgers. "And they certainly look more than fine, don't they?"

"The uniforms are made of cheap stuff, I'll wager," muttered Hi hoarsely. There was a choke in his throat over seeing his own nine so badly eclipsed in appearance by the despised Central Grammars.

Not less astonished were the Central Grammar boy spectators themselves. Not one, outside of the baseball squad, had known that any uniforms were to be worn on the field.

"Huh!" remarked Ted Teall, captain of the South Grammars, to one of his lieutenants. "We are the only school nine in town now without a uniform. When we get on the field to play we'll look like a lot of rag-pickers, won't we?"

"I know where they got 'em," choked Hi at last. "Their principal, Old Dut Jones, wouldn't see his boys look too badly compared with us, so he bought 'em as good uniforms as he could afford. It's a shame. That's what it is."

If Captain Dick and his baseball players walked rather proudly onto the field, it may have been partly due to the fact that they now knew that their uniforms were anything but "cheap." In point of fact, their uniforms had cost more than twice as much as those worn by Hi Martin's players.

"How did they get such uniforms?" That was the question that passed from lip to lip.

The answer was very simple, though as yet none of the onlookers knew what it was.

Not until one minute past four did the Central Grammar players know anything about the uniforms. Old Dut had dismissed the rest of the school, detaining Dick's players.

"Young men, we shall now hasten up to Exhibition Hall," announced the principal. He marched them up there, where they found the smiling Mr. Brown, backed by an assistant. Several boxes, opened, lay upon the floor.

"Now, young men," called Mr. Brown jovially, "let us see how quickly you can take your baseball uniforms and get into them."

"But what———" began Dick, then paused in absolute bewilderment.

"It's all right," Mr. Brown cheerily assured the dazed boys. "The uniforms are all paid for——won't cost you a cent."

"But you——you told us," protested Captain Dick Prescott, "that you were collecting measurements of members of schoolboys' baseball clubs."

"Well, that's the truth," protested Brown, with a mock air of injured innocence. "I'm a traveling salesman for the Haynes Sporting Goods Company, one of the biggest baseball outfitting companies in this part of the country. It's my business to travel and take orders."

"But we didn't give you any orders," gasped Dave.

"Some one did," laughed Mr. Brown.

"Who did?" blurted Tom Reade.

"Did you, Mr. Jones?" cried Dick.

"Not I," laughed the principal. "But I'll tell you, boys, who did. Prescott, you remember Mr. Winthrop, who is acting for Colonel Garwood in trying to find the latter's son? Amos Garwood hasn't yet been found, but Mr. Winthrop is satisfied that they are close at his heels, and that they will soon find him. Colonel Garwood is a very wealthy old man, and very fond of his missing son. Mr. Winthrop inquired how he could best serve the boys who had brought him the first word. Some one, I believe it was Len Spencer, the 'Blade' reporter, told about your not having uniforms. Mr. Winthrop wired the Haynes Company, placing an order for the best of uniforms, provided they could be finished to be delivered this afternoon. And here they are."

"When do you youngsters play?" called out Brown laughingly. "To-day or some other day?"

"I would recommend you to make good time," Old Dut urged. "You don't want to start the season by being late, do you. Besides the North Grammar boys might then claim the game by default."

That was enough to set Dick Prescott and his dazed comrades at work in earnest.

The uniforms were of blue, and of fine texture. Even baseball shoes had been provided. The stockings were blue. Then came the trousers. The blue jersey shirts bore proudly in front two golden letters each, "C.G." This inscription stood, of course, for "Central Grammar." Then there were coats of blue, to slip on over the jersey shirts; caps of blue and belts of blue, the latter edged with golden yellow to match the shirt initials.

Besides there were a catcher's mask, gloves for the different field players, half a dozen baseballs and an even dozen of bats.

"Finish dressing as quickly as you can," urged Old Dut. "Your time is slipping away."

At last they were ready. Carrying masks, bats, gloves, they fell in by twos, Principal Jones marching them from the building, along the street and into the field where their arrival had created such a furor.

Yet, excited as he was, Dick had not forgotten to ask both Mr. Brown and Old Dut not to fail to express their deepest thanks to Mr. Winthrop and to Colonel Garwood.

Ben Tozier, of the High School baseball nine, had been accepted as umpire for the day. He now came forward to meet Captain Dick's company.

"My, but you youngsters look about the finest ever," announced Ben. "I hope you can play as well as you look. Captain Prescott, do you claim any time for practice?"

"Not if it's time to begin playing," Dick answered.

"Yes; it is. I'll call Martin, and you two will attend me for the pitch of the coin."

"Wait a moment, please," called Hi, from across the field.

"What's the matter?" shouted a spectator.

"The North Grammars want to go home and change their uniforms," shouted another onlooker.

There was a great laugh at this, which caused Hi Martin to color and look belligerent. He came stalking across the field.

"Ladies and gentlemen," shouted Ted Teall, affecting the manner of an announcer, "I beg to state that the game about to begin will be between two famous nines, known as the Gentlemen and the Chromos."

At this there was more laughter, while Hi Martin shook with rage. Looking at the bright red so prominent in the North Grammar uniforms, there could be no doubt as to which nine had been dubbed the "Chromos."

"Mr. Umpire," called Hi angrily, "have you power to preserve order here to-day?"

"I'll do my best," agreed Tozier. "But this is an open field that any one may enter, and there are no police here."

"Play ball, you red-heads!" jeered a boy, referring to the bright red caps of the North Grammars. "Don't holler for the police until you find out whether you can stand up to the Centrals."

"Now, let us stop all guying of the players and all other nonsense," called Tozier firmly, as he held up his right hand. "Remember that we are here to see a game and not to listen to cheap wit."

That held the unruly ones back for a few moments. Tozier drew a coin from one of his pockets, exhibited it to the captains, and asked:

"Who will call the toss?"

"Martin may," nodded Captain Dick.

"Ready, then."

Ben Tozier sent the coin spinning skyward. When it turned to fall Hi called out:

"Tails."

"Heads win," declared Umpire Tozier.

"Captain Martin, have you any choice?" inquired Prescott politely.

"I didn't win the toss," Hi returned sulkily.

"But we'll give you your choice if you have any," Dick insisted.

"We'd rather go to bat," Hi observed.

"Then, Mr. Umpire," continued Dick, turning to Tozier, "the Centrals choose the field."

"Get to your places," nodded Ben. "Martin at bat; Percival on deck," called the score-keeper.

Dick ran down to the pitcher's box, while Greg, slipping on mask and glove, took up his position behind the plate.

Tozier carelessly broke the seal on the package enclosing a ball, inspected it, and dropped it into Dick's hands. Dick threw an overshoot to Greg, who mitted it neatly.

But Ted Teall could not let the occasion go by without some nonsense.

"Whack!" shouted Teall. "Woof! Did you hear it strike? And it hurt, too. Who has the arnica bottle?"

There was laughter, but Dick ignored it, sending in a neat drive over the plate. Greg caught it and sent the ball back.

As it once more reached Dick's hand Umpire Tozier shouted:

"Ready! Play ball!"

Greg Holmes signaled what he wanted. Dick gave the ball a twist, and the game was on.

Chapter V

"Say, dress a kid up swell, and send him on the street—-did you ever know him to be any good?" demanded Ted Teall scornfully of those who stood near him. "Well, that's what ails the Centrals. They're wearing a bale of glad dry goods and they can't keep their eyes off their togs long enough to find the ball."

Dick and Dave heard this as they went to grass at the end of the third inning.

So far, though the Centrals had made some bases, none of their players had succeeded in scoring at the plate. One of Hi Martin's players had scored a run in the first inning and another in the third.

"Teall is a torment, isn't he?" whispered Dick.

"He is now," muttered Dave. "He won't be after this game is finished."

"Why not?"

"I'm going to trim some of the funny talk out of him after the game."

"Don't do anything foolish, Dave," urged Dick.

"That won't be foolish. It's necessary."

"Don't do it, Dave, or even think of it. You'll give the Centrals the name of not being able to stand defeat."

Then Dick ran over to the box to begin pitching for the fourth inning. His arm had not given out. Prescott had been doing some pretty good pitching, and Greg had backed him up well. But the North Grammars had a few batsmen who seemed to guess the ball in advance.

"Hey, Mr. Umpire," shouted a boyish onlooker, as Dick faced the plate, ball in hand, "better call the game and let the Centrals play some weak primary school team."

Even at this cheap witticism there was considerable laughter.
It made Dick's face flush.

"I'll show 'em whether we can play or not," he muttered to himself, as he caught the signal from Greg. "We've got to start, too, for we've got to match those two runs and then pick up this game for our own."

Hi Martin was again at the plate. He swung his bat idly, grinning mockingly at Prescott.

"I'll let you off without trying, if you'll give me second base," offered Hi tantalizingly.

"If the batsman talks again he will be ordered off the grounds," declared Umpire Tozier sternly.

But Dick felt the sting of his opponent's taunt and longed to be even. Greg signaled for a drop ball—-a difficult one for a schoolboy to throw. It was the first time in the game that Greg had asked for this.

Dick "made up" the ball with extra care, then let it go. It looked like a chest-high ball as it came, and was so slow that Hi threw back his bat to slam it.

"A home run on this!" thought Hi exultantly.

From the sides of the field came a mocking laugh, for the ball had dropped, leaving Hi pounding wildly at the air.

"Strike one!" called Ben Tozier, slipping a pebble to his other hand.

Dick smiled quietly as the ball came back to him. Greg signaled for an outshoot. But Dick "made up" the ball and imitated his delivery of the throw before.

"I'll get down and get it, this time!" flashed Martin resentfully.
He did, only to find himself no nearer the ball than before.

"Strike two!"

Tittering came from the sides now, also some applause. The spectators had just begun to understand that Dick Prescott was pitching better ball.

"Ball one!"

Hi felt a bit better for a moment. Then:

"Strike three! Out!"

With a muttered growl of disgust, Captain Martin gave up his post to Percival.

"What has got into Prescott?" demanded Rodgers, of the Norths, anxiously.

"Oh, we'll pound him to pieces soon," muttered Hi.

"Strike one!" sounded the umpire's steady, low voice.

In a moment or two more it was: "Strike three. Out!"

Then a third batsman took post. Dick Prescott, his face now flushed with pleasure, not humiliation, and his eyes flashing battle, put the third man out for the Norths.

Yet, though the Central Grammars put two of their men on bases, they, too, went back to grass ere a run could be scored.

The fifth inning was almost a duplicate of the fourth; no ground gained. In the sixth, after having two men struck out, the Norths took two base hits away from Prescott, and had men on first and second. In an unwary moment for the Centrals the man at second made third just ahead of the ball.

"We'll have a third run in a moment, if our boys keep their heads," murmured Hi Martin confidently. "That will keep us at three to nothing."

At that instant Dick delivered a ball that the North batsman tapped, but just hard enough to drive it for a fair catch into Prescott's hands.

"You idiot!" glared Martin at the offender, as the Norths took the field.

However, all predictions were still in favor of the North Grammars, who had two runs put away while they had kept Prescott's men from scoring.

"Fellows, we've got to do something, and we must make it strong!" muttered Dick, as his side came in.

Reade went to bat—-was struck out.

"That wasn't very strong," sighed Tom, as he passed Dick going to the plate.

Dick Prescott had his favorite bat in his hand. He gripped it a little harder for an instant, then relaxed and waited for Hi's puzzling delivery.

"Strike one!"

Dick swung for the next one that came. Almost mechanically Tozier opened his mouth to call:

"Stri——-"

But Dick's willow cut in with a "whack!"

"Woof! Whoop!" Central boys among the spectators sent up an expectant yell, then watched breathlessly. Was the luck about to change?

"Go it! Go it! Go it!" yelled the Central boys in three different pitches of enthusiasm.

Dick, as he struck first and turned, took a fleeting look at the North's right fielder, still in pursuit of the long fly that had gone by him and was rolling over the field. Then, straining lungs and nerves, Dick sprinted toward the second bag.

"Go it! Hustle!"

Behind him Dick heard the whistle of the coming ball. Just ahead of him was the plate. He took a long leap, then slid. Second baseman held up the ball in his right hand.

"Safe, safe!" yelled the gleeful Central spectators.

"Out! That was out!" hoarsely declared the boosters for the North Grammars.

"Safe at second," called Ben Tozier steadily.

"Oh, you ape of an umpire!" grunted Hi Martin disgustedly, as he mitted the ball from second. For an instant he watched Dick, who was edging away from second. Then he turned to send in a drive past Greg, who now hovered over the plate.

Greg Holmes went to two strikes and three balls, Hi all the time alertly watching Prescott at second.

Crack! And now Greg was running. Norths' left-fielder muffed the ball, then recovered and threw like a flash to third. But Dick was there a shade of a second ahead of the leather.

"Safe" declared the umpire.

Hi Martin flashed a warning look at the catcher for his nine, then sent a sweeping glare around the bases. Greg and Dick smiled sweetly back.

"Play ball!" ordered Umpire Tozier.

Dan Dalzell was now at bat, tingling with anxiety, though his grin seemed a yard wide.

"Oh, you Danny Grin! Eat the leather!" appealed a Central rooter from the side.

Dan grinned again, his look seeming to say, "Watch me!"

Two strikes, with no called balls. Dick, dancing away from third, felt himself on tenterhooks. Not all of his perspiration was due to the heat of the day.

Again Dan offered. Crack! A wild, gleeful whoop went up from some of the Central rooters, while others held their breath. The ball went high, and right field came running in for it. As it happened, the fielder underestimated the length of the flight. It struck the ground to his rear and rolled. Before the outfielder could pick it up Dan had kicked the first bag.

"Prescott! Prescott!"

Dick was in, scoring the first run, while Greg was at second, and Dan hugging first as though he dared not be found two yards away from that bag.

Henderson now went to bat, accompanied by the grave anxiety of the members of his nine, for Spoff was not one of the star players. True to expectations Spoff struck out.

"Do it, Hazelton! You've got to do it!" yelled the Central fans despairingly. "Don't miss any tricks!"

Harry, however, could find nothing safe to hit at. He took first on called balls, advancing Greg to third and Dan to second.

Wrecker Lane now swung the willow. On his face was a do-or-die, dogged expression. Wrecker was not a brilliant player, though he was one to whom defeat came hard.

"Go after it, Wrecker. Put it over hard! Slam!"

After two strikes and one ball had been called Wrecker let go in deadly earnest. Bang! The blow split the leather, which went in an erratic though by no means short course. Greg dashed in over the plate amid wild cheers. Dan, hotfooting as he had never before done in his life, crossed the plate also. Wrecker, panting, reached first, looked at the fielder almost on the ball, sped on, then prudently turned and make back for first.

Toby Ross now went to bat, and struck out in crisp one-two-three order.

"Wrecker, that was a bully liner!" glowed Dick, grasping the hand of the boy who had saved the score in its critical moment. "You seemed to have Hi Martin's delivery down to a certainty."

"Yes, and it was a wonder, too," confessed Wrecker, still a bit dazed. "I couldn't see the ball at all, but I knew that it was up to me to do something."

"How do you feel now, Chromos?" bawled Ted Teall at the beginning of the seventh.

The score was now three to two in favor of Central Grammar.

It was still there when the seventh ended, and also at the finish of the eighth. Then the North Grammars went to bat for the first half of the ninth.

"You fellows simply must do something——do a lot," had been Hi's almost tearful urging as be addressed his fellows at the bench.

It was Bill Rodgers who stood before him as Dick twirled the ball, awaiting Greg's signal, which came a second later——a drop ball.

Bill swung for it, then looked foolish. Two more bad guesses, and he was out.

A second man was soon out, and then a third. Not one of the trio had been able to judge Dick's ball.

Central Grammar had won the first game by the close score of three to two. That, however, was as good for all purposes as any other could possibly be.

"What ails you Norths?" amiably remarked Ted Teall. "Is it the gayness of your uniforms? The red gets in your eyes and keeps you from seeing the ball."

"You're not funny," glowered Hi Martin. "You're merely a clown."

"Wait until my nine plays yours," retorted Teall genially. "Then we'll see who looks more like a clown——-you or I."

But now there was time, and Dick Prescott and his fellows had to tell scores of eager inquirers how they came by their new uniforms, when they had not expected to have any.

"Just what I thought, or as bad, anyway," muttered Martin when the news was brought to him. "These muckers couldn't buy their uniforms, as our fellows did. They had to depend upon charity to make a good appearance on the field."

"Hold on, there, Martin," angrily objected one of the Central fans. "I suppose it was charity, too, when you gave our fellows the game, eh? It was mighty kind of you, too."

"Huh!" retorted Hi. "This is only one game lost, and by a hair's breadth. Wait until the end of the season, and see who carries the laurels."

"Prescott, what do these letters mean on your jersey?" asked Ted Teall, halting and squinting at the golden yellow emblems.

"C.G.?" smiled Dick. "That's for Central Grammar, of course. But the letters have been put on so that they can be easily changed around to read G.C."

"What'll that stand for?" quizzed Teall, winking at some of the other fellows.

"Why, we'll change the letters around after we've played this series, and then the letters will stand for Grammar Champions."

"Oh, I see," grinned Ted. "My, but that will be kind of you, to give our fellows the jerseys."

"You haven't won them yet," retorted Dick. "The Centrals will keep their own jerseys and wear the G.C. by right of conquest."

"Perhaps they will, and perhaps they won't," muttered Hi Martin angrily to himself and Tom Percival.

Chapter VI

Saturday morning, about eight o'clock, the entire team of the Central Grammar met at Dave Darrin's house. In the front yard they waited for their captain.

"Queer Dick should be a bit late," muttered Tom Reade. "He's our model of punctuality."

"You'll see him come around the corner 'most any minute," Greg predicted.

Nor was Holmes wrong in this. When Prescott arrived he came on a jog trot.

"We wondered what kept you, our right-to-the-minute captain," announced Dave.

"Well, you see," replied Dick quizzically, "I've been thinking."

"Thinking?" repeated Tom. "Oh, I understand. You've been thinking about what the man on the clubhouse steps said."

"Well, hardly anything as big as that," teased Dick. "I'm afraid that you fellows are growing impatient on what is, after all, not a very important matter."

"So, then, the speech of the man on the clubhouse steps wasn't very important?" inquired Tom, seeking to pin their leader down.

"Why, that would depend on how you happened to regard what the man on the clubhouse steps said," Dick laughed.

"Is that what you're going to tell us?" almost bowled Hazelton.

"I don't know that I am going to tell you much of anything," Prescott continued.

"What did the man on the clubhouse steps say?" asked Dan, advancing with uplifted bat.

"You'll never drag the secret from me by threats or violence," retorted Dick, with a stubborn shake of the head.

"We're getting away from the point," Tom went on. "You said you had been thinking."

"Well?"

"You've made the claim of having been thinking, but you haven't offered the slightest proof."

"What I was thinking, fellows, was that we are obliged to meet the South Grammar nine on the diamond to-day."

"We're not afraid of them," scoffed Dave.

"No," Dick went on, "but I've an idea that we're up against an ordeal, after a fashion. You all know what a guyer Ted Teall is——how he nearly broke up our match with the Norths last Wednesday afternoon."

"Ted can't do any guying this morning," declared Greg readily. "If he does, the umpire will rule him out of the game, and that would snap all of Ted's nerve. No; Ted won't guy us to-day."

"But I'll tell you just what will happen to us," Dick offered. "The spectators who come from the South Grammar aren't under the umpire's orders. You may be sure that Ted has posted the fellows from his school on a lot of things that they can yell at us. Oh, we'll get guyed from the start to the finish of the game."

"If they go too far," hinted Dave, "we can thrash some of the funny ones afterwards."

"I shan't feel like thrashing anyone for having a little fun with us," remarked Reade.

"Thrashing wouldn't do any good, anyway," Dick continued. "Besides which, we might just happen, incidentally, to be the fellows that got the worst thrashing if we started anything like that going. I don't object to good-natured ridicule. But the South Grammar fellows may have some things to yell at us that will rattle our play. That's what I want to stop."

"How can you stop it?" queried Greg.

"That's what kept me home a little later than I intended to stay there," Dick replied. "I have been thinking, since last night, how I could take some of the starch out of Ted Teall, and have some way of throwing the horse laugh back on the South Grammar boys in case they start anything funny enough to rattle us."

"How did the thinking get on?" Tom wanted to know.

"I believe I've something here that will do it," Prescott replied, taking an object from one of his pockets and holding it up.

"It looks like a home-made ball for babies to play with," remarked Dan Dalzell, grinning.

"It's a home-made ball, all right," Dick nodded. "Yet I don't believe that I'd let a baby have it to play with."

"What's the matter with it?" Tom asked. "Loaded?"

"Some one told you," protested Prescott, pretending to look astounded.

"What are you going to do with that thing?" Dave insisted.

"If I have a chance I'm going to get Ted Teall up in the air, and before the crowd, too," Dick asserted.

"With this ball?" Greg asked, taking it from his friend's hand.

"Yes."

"Hm! I don't see anything about it to shatter the nerves of a hardy youth like Ted Teall," Greg muttered. "This ball is just wound with string and covered with pieces of old glove. Why, it's so soft that I don't believe I could throw it straight."

Greg raised the home-made ball to throw it.

"Here! Don't toss it, or you may put it out of business," objected Prescott, taking it away from his friend.

"If the ball can't be thrown, then what on earth is it good for?" questioned Darrin.

"I'll come to that by degrees," Dick promised. "Did you know that dad has secured a license this year to sell fireworks at his store?"

"Yes," nodded several of the boys.

"Well, yesterday, Dad had a lot of samples come in from the manufacturers. There were a few of the extra big and noisy torpedoes," Dick explained. "I got one of them and wrapped this string and leather around it."

Then, in low tones, Dick confided to his comrades the use to which he hoped to put the ball. There were a good many grins as the plot dawned on the young diamond enthusiasts.

"That'll be a warm one, if it works," grinned Reade.

"Say, but I shall be hanging right around to see it happen," declared Darrin.

Originally this Saturday game had been scheduled for two in the afternoon. However, so many of the schoolboys in town wanted to have Saturday afternoon for other fun that the time had been changed to nine in the forenoon.

"Hadn't we better be starting?" asked Dick, looking at his watch.

"Yes; I want to be in at the death of Teall," agreed Reade.

All in uniform the Central Grammars started down the street, though this time they did not march. As they moved along other boys joined them, some from the Central and others from the North Grammar. By the time that Dick's nine and substitutes neared the field more than a hundred fans trailed along with them.

Nearly three hundred other boys were walking about on the field, or lying down under the trees.

Already the South Grammar boys were on the field, practicing by way of warming up.

"Hello! Here come the bluebells!" yelled a group of South Grammar fans and rooters.

"Blue? You bet they'll be blue when the game is over!"

"Hey, Prescott! What'll you take for the letters on your shirt?"

"Gimme that yellow curl over your forehead? I saw it first."

"Oh, my, don't the Little Boys Blue look sweet?"

In silence the Central players marched by their tormentors. Dick gazed across the field to see Ted Teall swinging a bat at the home plate.

"Teall!" called Dick, as he and the others dropped their jackets at the batters' benches.

"Hello!" returned Ted. "I'm glad to see that you fellows really had the nerve to come to-day."

"I saw you doing some pretty wild batting, Teall," laughed Dick Prescott. "That kind of work won't save you when I get started. Shall I throw you in a few real ones—-hard ones—-before we get at it in earnest?"

"Go on!" retorted Ted scornfully.

"Oh, I won't hurt you," Prescott promised.

"You bet you won't," boasted Teall.

"He's afraid, even before the game starts," jeered a group of Central Grammar boys. "That's right, Ted. Guard your life."

"Don't be afraid, Teall," Dick urged tantalizingly. "Trying to hit some of my deliveries will be something like an education for you."

"Bosh!" sneered Teall.

"Then why won't you try a few?"

"I will, if you really think you can throw a ball that will rattle me any," Teall agreed, grinning broadly.

"Go at him, Dick!"

"Whoop! Show him what a cheap batter he is."

Laughing, balancing a ball in his hands, Dick glided out on to the diamond.

"Ready, Ted? Just see what you can do with one like this," Dick mocked.

It was a swift ball, but a straight one. To a batsman of Teall's skill it was not a difficult one to hit. Ted swung his bat and gave the ball a crack that sent it far out into outfield.

"Is that the best you can do?" jeered Ted.

"Oh, I've one or two better than that," replied Dick, pretending to feel flustered.

Again Prescott sent in a swift one, and once more Teall sent the leather spinning over the field. Hoots and cat-calls from the Souths filled the air. The Central fans began to look a bit uneasy. What was their champion pitcher doing, to let Teall get away with his deliveries as easily as this?

A third ball Dick drove in, with the same result as before.

"Say, what you fellows need is practice," leered Ted.

"Look out that I don't catch you yet," mocked Dick Prescott, bending to scoop up the returning ball from the ground. Then he wheeled like a flash to confront the batsman.

This time, by a quick substitution, Dick held the home-made ball.
He twirled it for an instant, then sent it in toward the plate.

"Just—-as—-easy!" scoffed Ted, whirling his bat, then reaching out for the ball.

Crack! Teall hit it soundly.

Bang! With such force had the batsman struck that he exploded the large torpedo inside the home-made ball. There was a rattling explosion, and Teall, unable to figure, in that first instant, what had happened, sent the bat flying.

"Ow-ow-ow!" yelled startled Ted, leaping up into the air. When he alighted he ran a dozen or more steps as fast as he could go, then halted and looked around him. For an instant Teall's face expressed panic.

Then mocking laughter from hundreds of throats greeted him.

"I knew any little thing out of the ordinary would rattle you," smiled Dick. "Don't lose your nerve. It wasn't anything."

"Just a fresh idiot's attempt to be funny!" growled Teall, his face now red with mortification.

"Laugh, Ted, confound you!" urged Tom Reade. "Laugh! Don't be a grouch."

"What you need, Teall," teased Dave Darrin, "is some nerve tonic. You ought not to let yourself get into such bad shape that you almost faint when you hit the ball."

For once Ted Teall's ready tongue went back on him. He could think of nothing to say that would not make him look still more ridiculous.

"I guess he'll be good, for one game at least," grimaced Dick as he turned to his teammates.

Chapter VII

The game had gone into the third inning, with the Centrals retired from the bat and the Souths now in from the field.

In the second inning Greg, backed splendidly by Tom and Dick, had scored a run for his side—-the only run listed as yet.

In this third inning, with South Grammar now at the bat, two men were out, and one on second when Ted Teall stepped to the plate.

"Put a real slam over on 'em, Ted!" shouted a South fan.

"Drive a ball over into Stayton and then fill up the score card while the Centrals are looking for it!" advised another Teall partisan.

"Centrals?" jeered another boy from the South. Grammar. "Centrals? Show 'em they're just plain hello-girls!"

Ted grinned broadly at this "hello-girls" nickname. Just then another fan from the southern part of Gridley piped up:

"Ted, eat 'em. They're only nine pieces of blue cheese!"

That was going too far, and it was time for Central Grammar to take notice effectively.

"Bang!" roared one half of the Central fans.

"Ow-ow-ow!" yelled the other half of the Central boosters, leaping up into the air.

Even Ted Teall had to laugh at this mortifying reminder of his terror when he had struck the torpedo ball. The next instant his face went deep red, for everyone on the field appeared to be laughing and jeering at him.

"Confound Prescott and his tricks!" muttered Teall under his breath. "It'll take a lot of thinking for me to get even with that trick."

Whizz-zz! went the ball by Ted's body, just below shoulder-high.

"Strike one!" called the umpire sharply.

"Centrals will get me rattled with that bang-ow-ow! of theirs every time they spring it on me," thought Ted savagely.

"Strike two!"

Again Ted had failed to realize that the ball was coming. In his anger be wondered whether he'd rather throw his bat at the umpire or at smiling Dick Prescott.

"Strike three!" called the umpire's steady voice. "Side out."

Then Ted, in sheer exasperation, did hurl his bat a score of feet away.

"Bang!" came in a volley of Central voices.

"Ow-ow-ow!" wailed the other half of Old Dut's boys while the North Grammars joined in.

"Go it, you boobs!" muttered Ted, shaking his fist at the spectators.

"Hurrah!" cheered Spoff Henderson from the subs' bench. "We know how to stop Ted Teall's mouth now!"

Teall happened to hear the remark.

"Oh, you fellows are a lot of boobies!" sputtered Ted wrathfully.

"Anyway," Toby Ross leered back at him, "we're not so young that we yell when we hit a ball by mistake."

In the fourth and fifth innings the Central Grammars, though they booked some base hits, did not succeed in getting any runs through. However, they succeeded in preventing Teall's nine from scoring, which kept the score still at one to nothing. In the first half of the sixth Harry Hazelton was brought home from third by a good one by Dan. Then the side went out. In this inning Teall again had a chance at bat. Before batting he stalked over to where a lot of his schoolfellows were grouped and muttered:

"Don't you fellows shoot any funny remarks in this inning. Keep quiet."

"Huh!" shot out one of the boys. "What's the matter with you, Ted?"

"No matter. But I don't want any funny line of talk steered over to the Centrals to-day."

"Seems to me you've changed a lot, Ted," grinned one of his classmates. "Yesterday afternoon you put us up to a lot of funny things to holler to-day."

"Forget 'em," ordered Ted.

"Dick Prescott certainly stabbed you with that torpedo," grinned another South. "Ted, your nerve is gone for to-day."

"Don't get too funny with me, or I'll see you after the game," threatened Teall, as he stalked away, for he was now on deck, and due to go next to bat.

The second man for the Souths struck out.

46

"Teall at bat!" called the score-keeper.

Hi Martin and a lot of the North Grammar boys had come to the field late. Hi didn't like to see the score two to nothing in favor of the Centrals. He would have preferred to have the Souths win.

"Let's get Prescott rattled?" whispered Martin.

"I don't believe you can do it," replied Bill Rodgers. "Prescott is a mighty cool one."

"Yes, we can," insisted Hi. "I'll tell you what to boiler just the instant that Teall picks up the stick and Prescott starts to twist the ball."

Ted, all unsuspicious, and believing that he had stilled his own band of teasing torments, picked up his bat and went to the plate.

"Put it over the robbers, Ted!" came from Hi Martin's crowd. "Don't be afraid of the Centrals—-the fellows who stole their uniforms from a lunatic in the woods."

Dick heard the senseless taunt and understood it. But it didn't anger or confuse him. Instead, the ball left his hand with surer guidance.

But a crowd of Central fans also heard, and imagined that the yell came from one of the groups of Souths.

"Bang! bang!" yelled a lot of Central Grammar boys with enthusiasm.

"Ow-ow-ow! Ow-ow-ow!" came the response.

"Strike one!" called the umpire. Ted, his face crimson and his eyes flashing fire, threw his bat from him.

"Teall, pick up your bat," ordered the umpire. "If you do that again I'll order you from the game."

"I don't care if you do!" trembled on Ted's lips, but he caught the words in time. He gulped, swallowed hard, hesitated, then went tremulously to pick up his stick. However, his grit was gone for the day. He struck out and retired.

"Ow-ow-ow!" yelled a few of the Central fans in the eighth, and Dave Darrin struck a two bagger, bringing Prescott in safe from second, scoring a third run and landing Darrin on second. Had not Ross struck out immediately afterward there would have been other runs scored. The count was now three to nothing in favor of the Central Grammars.

"Prescott's fellows are playing some ball," declared Bill Rodgers.

"Hub! You mean that the Souths don't know how to play," sneered Hi Martin.

"Teall's fellows are playing well," argued Rodgers. "If you watch, you'll see that the luck of the Centrals depends a lot on the way they run the bases. Whew! They go like greased lightning when they're sprinting around the diamond."

"Well, why shouldn't they run?" demanded Hi. "Prescott and his fellows have been running every day since the snow went away."

"I wish our Norths had been running all the time, too," sighed Bill.

The Souths were playing desperately well in the field. Dick's side came in for the ninth, but did not succeed in getting another run.

"Now, watch 'em closely, fellows," counseled Dick, as, from the benches, he started his men out to the field. "The Souths are mad and game, and they may get runs enough in this last half to beat us. Play, all the time, as if you didn't know what it was to be tired. Keep after 'em!"

Dick struck the first South Grammar fellow out. The next man at bat took first on called balls. The next hit a light fly that was good for a base. The player who followed sent a bunt that Dave, as short-stop, fumbled. And now the bases were full.

"Oh, you Ted!" wailed the South fans hopefully. "Do your duty now, Teall!"

Ted gripped the bat, stepping forward. As he reached the plate he shot at his schoolmates a look of grim resolution.

"I'll bring those three fellows in, if I have to kill the ball, or drive it through a fielder!" muttered Ted resolutely. "If we can tie the score then we can break this fearful hoodoo and win the game yet."

"Don't let that pitcher scare you, Ted!" yelled a South encouragingly. "He hasn't a wing any longer. It's only a fin."

"Codfish fin, at that," mocked another.

"Bang!" retorted a dozen Central fans.

Before the answering chorus could come Dick Prescott held up a hand, looking sternly at his sympathizers.

"Strike one!" called the umpire, and once more Teall reddened.

"I've got to brace, and work myself out of this," groaned red-faced Teall. "There's too much depending on me."

"Ball one!"

"Now, I hope the next one will be good, and that I can hit it a crack that will drive it into the next county," muttered Ted, feeling the cold sweat beading his forehead.

He judged wrongly, on a drop ball.

"Strike two!"

"Drive a plum into that pudding in the box, Ted," sang out one of his classmates.

"Ow-ow-ow!" shrieked a score of watching Central Grammar boys. That was the last straw. Ted felt the blood rush to his head and all looked red before him.

"Strike three! Side out! Game!" came slowly, steadily from the umpire. Then the score-keeper rose to his feet.

"Central Grammar wins by a score of three to nothing."

This time Ted Teall didn't throw his bat. Gripping it savagely, he stalked over to a group of his own schoolmates.

"What fellow was it that started the yelling?" demanded Ted huskily.

"Why?" challenged three or four of the Souths.

"I want to know who he is—-that's all," muttered Ted.

In a moment there was a mix-up. But Teall wasn't popular at that moment. A captain who had led his men into a whitewash was entitled to no very great consideration.

"Let go of that bat!" roared Ted, as he felt it seized. "Let go, or I'll hit some one with it."

"That's what he wants to do anyway," called out one of the boys. "Yank it away from him!"

The bat torn from him, Ted Teall was fighting mad. He was so ugly, in fact, that he was borne to the ground, three of his own classmates sitting on him.

"You're all right, Ted," announced one of his classmates. "All that ails you is that you've got a touch of heat. Cool off and we'll let you up."

"There's one guyer who has lost his hold on his favorite pastime of annoying other people," remarked Tom Reade grimly.

"Dick's trick was the slickest that ever I saw done in that line," chuckled Dave Darrin. "But I wonder how our fellows tumbled to the idea of calling 'bang' first, and then following it up with 'ow-ow-ow'?"

"Want to know very badly?" Tom questioned.

"I surely do," Darry nodded.

"Well, then," Tom declared, "I put some of the fellows up to that trick."

Chapter VIII

"I wonder what Ted Teall will do after this when he wants to play rattles on the other side?" inquired Harry.

Dick & Co. were now making the most of Saturday afternoon. Having no money to spend, and no boat in which to enjoy themselves on the river, they had gone out of Gridley some distance to a small, clear body of water known as Hunt's pond.

When sufficient time after dinner had passed, they intended to strip and go in swimming, for this pond, well in the woods, was, by common understanding, left for boys who wanted to indulge in that sport.

"I don't believe Ted will get very funny, in the immediate future," replied Tom reflectively. "His fellows came to the field, all primed with a lot of funny remarks they were going to shoot at us during the game. Yet the only fellows who got hit by any flying funny talk were the Souths themselves. I have been wondering if 'Bang——-ow-ow' was what cost the Souths the game?"

"I don't quite believe that," replied Dick. "Yet I am certain that it took a lot of starch out of Ted himself. Do you remember that time when he went over and spoke to his fellows?"

"Yes," nodded Greg.

"Well," Dick pursued, "I've heard since that that was the time when Ted went over and begged his fellows to 'can' all funny talk until the game was over."

"But they didn't," chuckled Dan.

"That was why Ted was so angry at the end."

"Anyway," Tom insisted, "Teall isn't likely to bother us any more."

"Either he'll quit on the funny talk," agreed Prescott, "or else he'll go to the other extreme and be more tantalizing than ever."

It would greatly have interested these Central Grammar boys had they known that the subject of their conversation was even then listening to them. Ted Teall, sore and angry, had come away from town all by himself. He wanted a long swim in the pond, to see if that would cool off the anger that consumed him.

Hearing voices as he came through the woods, Ted halted first, then, crawling along the ground, made his way cautiously forward. And now the captain of the South Grammar nine lay flat, his head hidden behind a clump of low bushes.

"Having fun over me, are they?" growled Ted.

"It was a rough trick to play, of course," laughed Dick. "But I felt so wholly certain Ted's fellows would start in to break us up that I felt I had to spring that torpedo trick in order to shut the other crowd up in advance."

"Oh, you did, did you?" thought Teall angrily.

"But now there's something else to be thought of," Prescott went on. "Teall is bound to feel sore and ashamed, and he won't rest until be has done his best to get even with us."

"Teall had better leave us alone," replied Tom, shaking his head. "Ted's brain isn't any too heavy, and he'll never be equal to getting the better of a crowd with a Dick Prescott in it."

"We won't do any bragging just yet," Prescott proposed.

"That's right. You'd better not," Ted growled under his breath.

"Fellows," announced Dan Dalzell, "I've made an important discovery."

"I wonder if he saw me?" flashed through Teall's mind, as he tried to lie flatter than before.

"Name the discovery," begged Hazelton.

"Look at your watches, fellows," Dan continued, "and I think you'll find that it's now proper time for us to go in swimming."

"So it is," Darrin agreed. "Hurrah!"

Little more was said for a few moments. All the fellows of Dick & Co. were busy in getting their clothing off.

"Say, but I hope you fellows get far enough away from your duds!" breathed Teall vengefully, as he watched through the screen of leaves.

"Do you fellows think we had better leave a guard over our clothes?" queried Dick, as they stood forth, ready for swimming.

"Not!" returned Dalzell with emphasis. "If I agreed to it, it would be just my luck to have the lot fall to me. For the next half hour I don't want to do a thing but feel the water around me all the way up to my neck."

"What's the use of a guard over our clothes?" queried Dave. "There isn't another soul besides ourselves in these woods this afternoon."

"Go on thinking that!" chuckled Teall.

Running out on a log and putting his hands together, Dick dived.

"How's the water?" called Tom.

"Cold," Prescott answered, blowing out a mouthful as he struck out for the middle of the pond. "You'd better keep out."

"He wants the pond all to himself," muttered Tom, and dived at once.

In a moment all six boys were in the water, sporting about and enjoying themselves.

"I wish they'd get further away from here," thought Ted wistfully. "They're hanging right around here. If I show myself they'll all swim in. There wouldn't be time to do anything."

All too late Ted heard some one coming through the woods behind him. He crouched, ready to crawl away to privacy, but found himself too late. Hi Martin parted the bushes as be forced his way through.

"Hello, Teall," called the North Grammar captain.

"Hush—-sh—-sh!" warned Ted, putting a finger to his lips.

"What's the matter?"

"Prescott and his crew are out there swimming, and their clothes are right below."

"I see," nodded Martin. "You want to get the clothes?"

"Sit down here, out of sight, and keep quiet, won't you?" urged Teall.

Hi sat down quietly. He didn't like Teall especially, but he disliked Prescott, and perhaps here was a chance to serve Dick's discomfort.

"If they'd only swim away for a little stretch!" whispered Ted.

"I see," nodded Hi Martin rather pompously. "Too bad, isn't it? Now, Teall, you and Prescott both come from mucker schools, and I don't know that I ought to butt in any. But I don't mind seeing you torment Prescott a bit. You wait. I'll go in, and maybe I can challenge those fellows to swim down the pond that will take them away from this point."

Ted's face had flushed sullenly at Hi's remark about "mucker schools." At another time Teall might have been ready to fight over a slighting word like that. Just now, however, he craved help against Prescott more than anything else.

"All right," urged Ted. "You decoy that crowd away from here for a few minutes, and maybe I won't do a thing to them!"

"I'll see what I can do for you," returned Martin, going down to the edge of the pond.

"How's the water, fellows?" called Hi.

"Fine," returned Dick withenthusiasm.

"Room enough in the pond for another?" Hi asked.

"Surely. Come on in."

"I believe I will," Hi answered, seating himself and fumbling at his shoe-lacings.

A couple of minutes later Hi dived from the log and swam out to the other boys.

"Are you fellows any good on swimming distances?" Martin asked, as, with lazy stroke, he joined Dick & Co. The North Grammar boy was an expert swimmer and proud of it.

"I guess we can swim a little way," Prescott replied. "I don't remember that we ever swam any measured courses."

"Can you swim down to that old elm?" asked Hi, indicating a tree at the further end of the pond.

"We ought to," smiled Dick.

"Come along, then," invited Hi, starting with a side stroke.

Dick & Co. started in irregular fashion, Darrin and Reade soon spurting on ahead of Martin.

"How long can you tread water?" inquired Hi, after they had reached the neighborhood of the elm.

This sport is always interesting to boys who are good swimmers. Forthwith some endurance tests at treading were started. Then Hi showed them all a few "stunts" in the water, some of which Dick & Co. could duplicate easily, and some which they could not.

Thus the minutes slipped by. Hi, for once in his life, went out of his way to be entertaining to Central Grammar boys. But, at last, he muttered to himself:

"I guess Teall has had plenty of time for his tricks. If he hasn't, then all afternoon wouldn't he time enough."

"Hello, Hi," called Dick. "Where are you going?"

"Back to dress," Martin replied. "I've been in long enough."

"I guess we all have," Dick nodded, himself turning back. His chums followed.

"I don't know whether I'll dress or not," remarked Tom Reade, as he shot ahead of the others. "If I find I don't want to dress, then I'll just sit on the bank and dry my skin before going in again."

Continuing his spurt, Tom kept on until be reached the log from which the first diving had been done. He waded ashore, looked about in some bewilderment, and then called over the water:

"Say, fellows, just where was it that we left our clothes?"

"Why, barely a dozen feet back of the log," Dick called from the water.

"Hardly ten feet from where my clothes lie," added Hi Martin, his face solemn, but with an inward chuckle over the rage of six boys that he knew was soon to follow.

"But where are your clothes, Martin?" asked Tom, staring about him. "Where is anybody's clothes?"

The look in Hi's face changed rapidly. He took a few swift, strong strokes that bore him to shore.

Then, indeed, Martin's wrath and disgust knew no bounds. For his clothing was as invisible as that of the Central Grammar boys.

Chapter IX

"Confound that fellow Teall!"

This angry expression slipped past Hi's lips unguardedly.

By this time Dick Prescott was on shore. His quick, keen glances took in the patent fact that some one had removed all the discarded clothing from sight.

"So Ted Teall was around here, and you knew that he was going to take our clothing?" demanded Dick, flashing a searching look at Hi Martin.

When too late, Hi Martin saw how he had put his foot into the mess by his indignant exclamation.

"And, knowing that Teall was going to slip away with our clothing," Dick went on, "you went into the water and lured us away to the lower end of the pond. That was what you did to us, was it, Martin?"

Hi shook his head, then opened his mouth to utter an indignant denial.

"Don't try to fool us," advised Dick bitterly. "Martin, you may have thought it funny, but it was a mean trick to serve us, and I am glad that Teall has shown you how little he likes you."

Under ordinary circumstances Ted might have left Hi Martin's clothes behind. It had been Hi's impolitic remark about "mucker schools" that had decided Ted to take away Hi's belongings as well.

"That Teall is a dirty sneak," cried Hi.

"He was simply a comical genius as long as he took only our clothes," Dick retorted. "But now that your things are gone as well, it's a mean, low-down bit of business."

"Martin," observed Tom Reade dramatically, "thine own ox is gored."

"Talking won't bring back any duds," grunted Harry Hazelton. "Teall can't have gotten very far with such a load. Let's rush after him."

"You lead the way, then, son," suggested Dick, "and instead of following you, we'll wait here until you bring the things back."

"I wonder which way he went?" puzzled Hazelton.

"Probably straight to the road," smiled Dick grimly. "That's the shortest cut, and the road isn't far from here."

"But I can't go near the road in this—-this—-fix," sputtered Harry, looking down at his wet, glistening skin.

"Exactly," nodded Prescott. "Nor can any of us go. That's the joke. Like it? Ha, ha, ha!"

Dick's laugh had anything but a merry sound. None of the boys had a truly jovial look, nor was it to be expected of them. Tom was solemn as an owl, Harry fussy; Dan was grinning in a sickly sort of way, as was Dave Darrin. Greg Holmes, utterly silent, stood with his fists clenched, thinking how he would like to be able at this moment to pounce upon Ted Teall.

"It's an outrage!" sputtered Hi Martin, white to the roots of his hair. He was walking about, stamping with his bare feet on the ground, the fingers of both his hands working nervously.

"Oh, well, you won't get any sympathy in this crowd," Tom assured Hi glumly. "You were party to this, and all that disturbs you is that any one should dare take the same kind of a liberty with you. We don't care what happens to you, now, Martin."

"What shall we do with Martin, anyway?" demanded Dan Dalzell.

"Nothing," returned Dick crisply. "He isn't worthy of having anything done to him."

"Let's call 'Ted' with all our might," proposed Harry.

"You can, if you want to," Dick rejoined. "I doubt if he is now near enough to hear you. Even if he did hear, he'd only snicker and run further away."

After a few moments more Dick and his chums, as though by common consent, squatted on the sand near the edge of the pond. It was warmer for them that way. Martin edged over close to them. Not one member of Dick & Co. did the captain of the North Grammar nine really like, but in his present woeful plight Hi wanted human company of some kind, and he could not very well go in search of people who wore all their clothing.

While the swimmers had been occupied in the water at the lower end of the pond, Ted Teall had been wonderfully busy.

First of all, Ted had loaded himself with about half the clothing belonging to Dick & Co. The shoes he had carried by tying each pair by means of the laces and swinging three pair around his neck. The first load be carried swiftly through the woods until be came to a thicket where he hoped he would find concealment.

Then he had gone back for the other half of the clothing. This, upon arrival at the thicket, Ted dropped in on top of the first installment.

"Now, I guess I ought to hide somewhere where there won't be the least danger of them finding me. Then I can see the fun when those fellows come ashore," chuckled Teall. "Hold on, though! There's one more debt to pay. That confounded Hi Martin called the South Grammar a 'mucker' school. I believe I'll hide his clothes, too, for his saying what he did. But I'll have to go carefully, and see whether the fellows are still out of sight."

Ted returned with a good deal of caution. Then he discovered, by the sound of voices, that the swimmers were still at the lower end of the pond.

"Plenty of time to get Hi's duds, too," chuckled the pleased joker. He slipped down close to the beach, gathering up all of Martin's garments and the hat and shoes.

"Say, it must be fine to have a pretty well fixed father," murmured Ted wistfully. "All these duds of Hi's are of the best quality. I wonder if I'll be able to wear clothes like these when I'm earning my own money?"

Then he started off, going more slowly than on his two previous trips, for he felt that he had plenty of time. But at last the nearing voices of the returning swimmers warned him.

"They can't see me," chuckled Ted. "If any of 'em chase me, I can make a quick dash for the road and they won't dare follow me there. They'd be afraid of running into other people."

So Ted even dallied for a while. Some of the angry words uttered reached his ears and delighted him.

"Hi Martin is hot with wrath, and I'm glad of it," chuckled Ted to himself. "So he thought I'd spare him, did he! Huh! The next time he'd better be a little more careful over his remarks about 'mucker' schools!"

Then Ted walked on again leisurely.

"I believe I'll let these fellows stay here until about dark, hunting for their clothes, and not finding 'em," reflected Teall. "Then I'll have Ed Payne drop around and tell 'em just where to look. They can't thump Payne, for he won't be guilty of anything but helping 'em. Then maybe Dick Prescott will pitch dynamite again for me to bat at!"

Teall gained the thicket that concealed the other clothing. Just as he was about to cast Martin's belongings after the other wardrobes, he was disturbed by a sound close at hand.

With a start Ted looked up. Then he felt uneasy; frightened, in fact. At his side stood a shabbily dressed man of middle age. The man's cheeks were sunken, though they burned with an unhealthy glow. There was, in the eyes, also a light that made Ted creepy.

"S-s-say, wh-what do you want?" stammered Teall.

"So you are a thief, and at work?" inquired the man, who had rested a thin but rather strong hand on Ted's shoulder.

"A thief?" Teall repeated indignantly. "No, sir! And nothing like it, either."

"Is all the clothing in there yours?" demanded the stranger sternly.

"No, sir," Ted answered promptly.

"Then———"

"You see," Ted went on more glibly, and trying to conceal the fact that he was very uneasy under those burning eyes, "it's just a joke that I'm playing on some fellows who are swimming."

"You consider that sort of a joke humorous?" demanded the stranger, tightening the grip of his hand on Teall's shoulder until the boy squirmed.

"It's not a bit worse than what one of them did to me this morning," Ted asserted, strongly on the defensive now. "And I don't know what business it is of yours, mister. Who are you, anyway?"

"My name," replied the other quietly, "is Amos Garwood."

"Amos Gar——-wood?" Ted repeated. At first the name conveyed no information to him. But suddenly he remembered the name that had been on everyone's tongue a few days before.

"The crazy man?" cried Ted, his voice shaking. Then the woods rang with his startled combination of whoop and prayer.

"This is no place for me!" gasped Teall huskily, as, frantically, he tore himself free of that grip on his shoulder.

Without more ado Ted Teall broke through cover for the road. Never before had he realized how fast it was possible for him to sprint. Terror is an unexcelled pacemaker at times.

That whoop, followed by the yell of fear, traveled until it reached the boys at the lakeside. The distance and the breeze must have robbed the voice of some of its terror, for Dick sprang to his feet like a flash.

"That was Ted Teall's fine voice!" he cried, running up the slight slope. "Come on, fellows! We'll travel straight in that direction——-and we'll find our clothing."

59

Nor were any of the boys very far behind Dick in the mad race. Though two or three of them stepped on stones on the way, no one gave a thought to so slight an accident.

Nor was it long ere they burst from cover and came upon Amos Garwood, standing as though lost in thought, for Garwood was trying to comprehend Teall's words, "the crazy man."

All in a flash Dick recognized the man. So did his chums. Hi Martin alone was in the dark.

"Good afternoon," was Garwood's greeting, as he looked up as though coming out of a trance. "You are looking for your clothing, I imagine?"

"Marvelous what a good guesser you are, sir," gasped Tom.

"You'll find your clothing in this thicket," announced Garwood, indicating the spot with a wave of one arm.

Dick and Tom piled into the thicket, passing out the mixed-up articles to the other boys. A quick sorting was made and each item claimed.

"Say!" cried Hi, greatly disturbed. "There isn't a single thing of mine here."

"Serve you right, then," uttered Tom, as he drew an undershirt over his head. "You don't deserve anything to wear."

"You fellows didn't hand out my things," uttered Hi, darting into the thicket. He searched savagely at first, then despairingly. Not a shred of his wardrobe was to be found.

"What became of my clothes?" Martin demanded, stepping out into the open. Tears brimmed his eyes now.

"Clothes? Your clothing?" asked Amos Garwood, again coming to a realization of things about him. "Why, I believe the boy who yelled and ran away from here carried one armful of things with him."

"Which way did he run?" throbbed Hi.

"That way." Garwood pointed to the road.

"You fellows get a few things on and run after Teall as fast as you can go," ordered Hi. "Quick! Don't lose a moment. Do you hear?"

"Yes," nodded Prescott.

"Hustle, then!"

"Forget it," requested Dick, deliberately drawing on a shoe over a sock, next doing the lacing slowly and with great care.

"Which one of you will go!" asked Hi, turning appealingly to the others.

"Hear the echo?" mocked Dave Darrin. "The echo says, 'which one?'"

"Say, you fellows are meaner than poison!" Hi exploded tremulously.

"You have a very short memory, Hi," retorted Greg Holmes.

"Who was it that put up the job on us? Who helped Teall to do it?" asked Harry Hazelton.

"But I'm sorry for that," protested Hi Martin, tears again coming to his eyes.

"I believe you," Dick nodded cheerily. "You're indeed sorry——sorry for the way it turned out for yourself."

"But aren't you fellows going after Teall and my clothes?" insisted the naked one.

"We're not going to chase Teall," Darrin answered, "if that's what you mean. But, see here, Martin, I'm not going to be downright mean with you."

"Thank you," said Martin gratefully. "You always were a good fellow, Darrin."

"I'm going to be a good fellow now," Dave pursued. "I'm not going to chase Teall, for we don't know which way he went, and he'll be hiding. But I'll go around to your house and tell your folks where you are, and what a fix you're in."

I'll go to-night, just as soon as I've eaten my supper."

"You——you great idiot!" exploded Hi.

"Now, for that insult, I take back my promise," Dave retorted solemnly. "You needn't talk any more, Martin. I won't do a blessed thing for you now."

"Dave, you're altogether too rough on a fellow that's in hard luck," remonstrated Greg, then turned to Martin to add:

"Hi, it's no use to go chasing Ted Teall, but I'll tell you what I'll do. I'm all dressed now, and I'll go straight to your house and get some clothes for you, so you can come out of these woods and walk home. I'll do it for half a dollar."

"Thank you, Holmesy, I'll do it," Martin eagerly promised. "And I'll thank you, too, from the bottom of my——"

"You can keep the thanks," proposed Greg gravely. "But you can hand over the half dollar."

"E-e-eh?" stammered Hi, nonplussed, rubbing one hand, for an instant, over his naked thigh in the usual neighborhood of the trousers' pocket.

"Fork over the half dollar!" Greg insisted. "This is a strictly cash-in-advance proposition."

"Why, you—-you—-you———-" stuttered Hi in his wrath. "How can I pay in advance when Ted Teall is a mile away from here with my—-my trousers and all?"

"Cash right in hand, or I don't stir on your job," insisted Greg.

"I—-I'll pay you a whole dollar as soon as I can get home," Hi offered eagerly.

"Hi Martin, after what you've done to us to-day," demanded Greg virtuously, "do you think there's a fellow in this crowd who'd take your word for anything? If you don't pay right now, then I won't stir a step for you."

Again tears of helpless rage formed in Hi's eyes. Amos Garwood stood looking on, unseeing. But Dick Prescott's thoughts were flying like lightning. He knew that, somehow, Garwood ought to be seized and held until the friends searching for him could be notified.

Chapter X

"You fellows seem to think that everything is done when you get your own old duds back," complained Hi Martin angrily. "You don't seem to think that there's any need of doing anything for me."

"Why should we?" demanded Dick curtly. "You're the fellow who helped put up a job to hide our clothes. Now, you yell because you can't find your own."

"I'll go and get you some other clothes, whenever I'm paid for it in advance," Greg smilingly repeated his offer.

Dick's brain was busy with plans for holding Amos Garwood until the latter's father and friends could take charge of him.

"You're all the meanest lot!" protested Martin, tears of anger standing in his eyes.

"And you're the funniest fellow," mocked Tom. "To see a lot of sport in playing a trick on us, but howling like a dog with a can tied to his tail when you find yourself the only one stung by the joke."

"I'm going to leave here," Dick suddenly declared.

"Oh, I wish you would find my clothes and bring them to me," begged Hi.

"Come along, Greg. You, too, Dave. The rest wait here until we come back."

Dick shot a significant look at Tom Reade, then glanced covertly in Amos Garwood's direction. Reade understood and nodded.

"I don't really need or want you along with me, Dave," Dick murmured as soon as the three boys were out of sight of the others. "What I wanted was a chance to talk to you. Amos Garwood must be held, if necessary, until we can find some men to seize him and turn him over to the authorities. Be careful and tactful with him, but don't let him get away from you. The other fellows will help you, if necessary. I'm taking Greg with me, just so that Greg may run in one direction and I in another, in case we don't find help easily. But you get back and help Tom and the others. Of course you won't lay hands on Amos Garwood unless it becomes necessary, but in any case don't let him get away from you. Now, hurry back, for, if Garwood suspects, and shows fight, it will take all four of you to hold him. But if you all talk naturally and pleasantly, I don't believe he will be suspicious, or make any effort to get away."

Dave nodded, turning back, while Dick and Greg hastened to the road. Barely had they turned into the highway, when, a short distance, ahead, they espied a boy standing under a tree.

"There's Ted, and he has Martin's clothes with him," called Dick quietly. "Let's hurry up to him and get him to take the clothes back."

"A precious lot I care whether Hi Martin ever has any clothes again," Greg retorted.

"Oh, well, Greg, there's such a thing as a joke, and there's such a thing as carrying it too far. Hi Martin has had his dose of punishment already. We can afford to be decent and let up on him now. Hi, there, Ted!"

Teall looked as though uncertain whether to run or to stand.

"Don't be afraid, Ted," Dick called pleasantly. "A joke is all right, and we admit that it was on us."

So Ted, after a first start of suspicion, decided to remain where he was.

"Hi Martin sent you after his duds, I reckon?" inquired Ted as the other two boys ran up to him. All of Hi's apparel lay on the ground near Teall's feet.

"He certainly wanted some one to come," laughed Dick. "But, say, Teall, the thing has been rubbed in too hard. Run back with the things. You'll find all hands where you hid our things."

"And I'll find the crazy man there, too, maybe," ventured Teall. "Also, I'll run right into a gang that is just waiting to trim me. I thank you kindly, but if any one is to go back into that crowd with Hi's things, it will be some one else. I won't go—-too much regard for my health, you know."

"Greg, you carry Hi's clothes back," urged Dick. "I'll take Ted with me."

"I will not," flared Greg in open revolt.

"Be a good fellow," begged Dick.

"That's all right," grumbled Greg Holmes. "But I'm no valet to any North Grammar boy.

"If you fellows won't either of you do it," protested Dick, "I'll have to do it myself, and—-oh, dear! I'm in such a hurry to get help to take care of Garwood."

"What about that crazy man, anyway?" demanded Ted, his mouth agape with curiosity.

"I don't believe he's crazy at all, though he may perhaps be a little flighty in his head," Prescott answered. "At any rate, he isn't violent. There's no danger in him. Ted, won't you take back these———-"

Teall shook his head with vigor.

In the meantime four Grammar School boys had stationed themselves around Garwood, who stood under a tree chewing a blade of grass. Hi, either from modesty or humiliation, had retired into a clump of bushes.

"They've gone to find that boy who took the clothes, I suppose," remarked Amos Garwood, looking towards Dave Darrin. "That was a strange boy, a very nervous boy," continued Garwood aloud. "Just as soon as I told him my name, he turned and fled like a streak of lightning. I wonder what ailed him?"

"I wonder?" repeated Dave solemnly.

"And that boy said something else that made me very curious," went on Amos Garwood. "He said something about a crazy man. I almost thought he referred to me, though the boy himself was the only one who showed any signs of being crazy. What did he mean?"

"He hasn't told us," Dave rejoined.

But Hi, who felt that he was being shamefully used by the crowd, suddenly broke in with:

"If your name is Garwood, then Ted Teall meant that you're the one that's crazy. And I know where the boys have gone. They're not looking for my clothes at all. They're looking for constables to come and seize you!"

"You shut up, Hi Martin!" raged Tom Reade, making a dash at Hi's leafy screen.

But the harm was done. Amos Garwood changed color swiftly.

"Ha, ha! Ho, ho!" he laughed harshly. "I begin to understand now. But no one shall seize me. I won't let any one take me."

He started madly through the bushes, not seeking a path. Dan, who was nearest him as be passed, leaped and threw both arms around the man, bringing him to the ground. Dave leaped to aid Dalzell, nor was Hazelton long in getting to the spot. Tom Reade decided to defer the punishment of Martin, and went to the aid of his friends instead.

Though he had been downed swiftly, Garwood was almost as speedily on his feet, fighting desperately. Darrin he seized and hurled several feet into a thicket. Dalzell sought again to wind his arms around the fellow's legs, but was brushed aside as though he had been a fly.

Tom Reade received a blow against his right shoulder that sent him reeling away, while Hazelton, in trying to get a new hold, was boxed over his left ear in a way that seemed to make the earth revolve about him.

Hardly had the scrimmage started when Garwood was free.

"No one shall stop me, or hinder me!" cried Amos exultingly, then wheeled and raced through the forest.

After him, as soon as they could recover their faculties, dashed the Grammar School boys. For a minute or two they had him in sight. Then Garwood, on his long legs, sped ahead and out of sight. For another half minute they could hear the man's progress through the brush. After that all was so still that Darrin and the others halted, gazing perplexedly at each other.

"Where is he?" gasped Tom.

"Which way did he go?" breathed Dan.

Though they listened, neither sight nor sound now aided them.

"Of all the sneaks and trouble-makers!" cried Dave Darrin indignantly. "Hi Martin ought to be tied to a tree and switched until he can't see! He's a regular babbling butt-in."

"What good did it do him to meddle in that fashion?" burst from Reade. "The mean, worthless fellow! And we had plenty of reason to feel grateful to Colonel Garwood, Amos's father, after the handsome uniforms that were given us."

"It must have been Hi's reason for spoiling our plan," muttered Hazelton. "He didn't want us to be able really to earn the uniforms."

"Come on," urged Dave. "We mustn't lose a bit of time. If we spread out and keep on we may sight Garwood again."

"Huh!" muttered Reade. "If Garwood has gone right ahead at the speed with which be started, then he's in the next county by this time. We won't see him again to-day."

After a few minutes of searching the other boys came to the same conclusion.

"Out into the road, then," ordered Dave, who naturally took command when Prescott was absent. "We want to head off any men Dick may have found and tell 'em what has happened."

They turned, making rapidly for the road. As it happened, they came out near where Ted Teall stood guarding Hi's clothing.

"Have you seen Dick?" was Darrin's hail. "Yes; he and Holmesy have run down the road to get some men. Here they come now with the men," Ted answered, pointing.

Dick had had the good fortune to find help before going far.
With such a reward as had been offered for the capture of Amos Garwood, it was not difficult to find men who could be interested in taking part in such a capture.

"What are you all doing here?" Dick yelled up the road.

"Garwood got away from us," Dave shouted back. "Hi Martin spoiled the game for us, and we simply couldn't hold Garwood."

Then Dick, Greg and the three men hurried up. Dave and Tom told the story.

"What a miserable hound Martin is!" burst from indignant Dick.

"So that boy spoiled us from getting a good slice of a fat reward, did he?" growled one of the three men. "Where is he?"

"Up in the woods," muttered Dick, "waiting until some one takes him his clothes. Ted Teall, you've simply got to return the booby's outfit to him."

"Won't do it," retorted Teall.

"But you took them away from him," Dick insisted.

"Suppose I did?"

"It may prove a serious matter, to steal any one's clothing," Prescott retorted. "And Hi Martin's father is a hot-tempered man. Ted, if I were in your place I don't believe I'd run the risk of being arrested. A joke is one thing, but keeping any one's clothes, after you've taken 'em, is proof of intention to steal. I don't believe I'd take the risk, if I were you."

The men were turning back down the road now, having decided to telephone the Gridley police and then turn out more men and go into the woods for an all-night search. Dick & Co. turned to go with the men.

"Say, you fellows," Ted called after them. "You going to shake me like that? Who's going back into the woods with me, if I take these clothes to Hi?"

"No one," Dick retorted over his shoulder. "You don't have to take the clothes back, you know, unless you happen to consider it safer to do it."

"Hang those fellows," sighed Ted, as be gazed after the retreating Dick & Co. "Well, I guess they've got me. The wise thing will be for me to take these duds to Hi before he catches cold."

So Ted gathered up the articles of apparel and with them started back into the woods.

"Hi, Hi!" he called, as be neared the thicket.

"Here," came an angry voice.

"Here's your old duds," growled Teall, as he reached the thicket that concealed young Martin, and threw the things on the ground.

"It's about time you brought 'em back," snapped Hi, making a dive for his belongings.

"I had a good mind not to do it at all," retorted Teall hotly.

"You'd have found yourself in hot water if you hadn't done it," Hi declared testily, as, having drawn on his underclothing, he seated himself to lace up his shoes. Then he rose and reached for his trousers.

"See here, Ted Teall," cried Hi suddenly, holding the trousers forward, "what did you do with my gold watch that was in the pocket of these trousers."

"I didn't see your old watch," grumbled Ted.

"Then you lost it out of the pocket while running through the woods, did you?" insisted Hi angrily.

Teall felt cold sweat come out on his neck and forehead. Well enough did he remember the gold watch, which was the envy of most of the schoolboys in Gridley. Nor was there any denying the fact that the watch was absent.

"Honest, Hi; honest," he faltered. "I didn't see the watch at all."

"You've got to find it, just the same," retorted Martin stubbornly. "If you take things away and lose them you've got to find them, or make good for them. Now, Mr. Smarty, I'm going home, and you're going to find the watch."

"Say, you might help a fellow and be decent about it," pleaded Ted.

"I didn't lose the watch, and I won't help you look for it," snapped back Hi Martin, as he strode away. "But if you aren't at my home with that gold watch before dark to-night, then you may look for things to happen to you! Find the watch, or wait and see what the law will do to you, Mr. Ted Smarty!"

Right on the spot Ted Teall started to look, a feeling of dull but intense misery gnawing in his breast.

"Oh, gracious! But now I've gone and done it!" groaned Teall, beginning to shake in his shoes. "Now, I'm in a whole peck and half of trouble, for I'll never be lucky enough to find that watch again!"

Chapter XI

Ted didn't find the watch, nor did the men searchers get anywhere near a reliable trail of Amos Garwood.

As for Dick & Co., they aided in the search for a while, then went home to supper, feeling that they had done their present duty as well as boys might do it.

Ted Teall slunk home considerably after dark. Fortunately, as it happened, his parents didn't force him to tell his reason for being late, but Ted sat down to a supper that was cold and all but tasteless. However, Teall could find no fault with his supper. He was so full of misery that he didn't have the slightest idea what the meal was like.

"I wonder if I'd better run away from home before I'm arrested?" puzzled Ted, as he secured his hat and stole away from the house. "Br-r-r-r! I don't like the idea of being hauled up in court."

It finally occurred to him that, if the officers were on his track, the news would be known up in town.

"If I nose about Main Street, but keep myself out of sight, and keep my eyes peeled for trouble," reflected wretched Ted, "I may find out something that will show me how to act."

So to Main Street Ted slowly made his way, keeping an alert lookout all the time for trouble in the form of a policeman.

At one corner Ted suddenly gasped, feeling his legs give way under him. By a supreme effort of will he mastered his legs in time to dart into a dark doorway.

"Huh! But that was a lucky escape for me," Teall gasped, as he came out from the doorway, peering down the street after the retreating form of Hi Martin's father. "I guess he's out looking for me. He'll want his son's gold watch. Crackey! I wonder if folks will think I'm low enough down to steal a fellow's watch?"

If Teall was rough, he was none the less honest, and had all of an honest boy's sensitive horror of being thought guilty of theft.

"Yet the matter stands just this way," Ted reflected as he moped along. "The watch must have been in the trousers when I snatched 'em up, and the watch wasn't there when I returned the trousers. What will folks naturally think? Oh, I wonder if there ever was as unlucky a fellow in the world before?"

A great lump formed in Ted's throat as he puzzled over this problem.

"Hello, Teall!" called a hearty voice. "Was Hi much obliged when you gave him back his duds this afternoon?"

Dick Prescott was the speaker, and with him were his five chums.

"Nothing like it," muttered Ted, turning as the boys came up. "Say, something awful happened to-day, and I'm in a peck of trouble!"

"Tell us about it," urged Tom Reade.

Ted started to tell them, mournfully.

"I don't believe a word of that, Ted," Dick broke in energetically.

"I'm telling you just as it happened," Teall protested.

"Oh, I guess you are, all right. But I don't believe Hi had his watch with him. If he had had it, he would have worn a chain or a fob, and I didn't see any, did you, fellows?"

"If I thought he had fooled me———-" muttered Ted vengefully. Then, with a change of feeling, he continued:

"But I don't believe he was fooling me. Hi was too mad, and he looked as though he'd like nothing better than to see me get into big trouble over it."

"You went all over the ground where you'd been?" Dick asked.

"Must have gone over it seventeen times," Ted declared positively. "I didn't quit looking until it was so dark that my eyes ached with the strain. But not one sight did I catch of the watch."

"Don't worry any more about it, Teall," urged Dave Darrin. "Like Dick, I don't believe, for an instant, that Hi had his watch with him."

"Here comes Hi now, out of the ice cream place," whispered Greg.

Young Martin certainly didn't look much worried as he gained the street. For a few seconds he looked about him. He saw Dick & Co. and scowled. Then he caught sight of Ted, despite the latter's trying to shrink behind Reade.

"See here, Teall, did you find my watch?" demanded Hi, stepping over to the group. His manner was aggressive, even threatening.

"N-n-no," stammered Ted.

"Then I don't believe you looked for it," insisted Hi.

"Didn't I, though? Until after dark," Ted rejoined.

"Then why didn't you find it?"

"Because I didn't happen to see it— -that was the only reason," Teall retorted.

"There may have been another reason," observed Hi Martin dryly.

"Do you mean to say that I tried to steal it?" flared Ted, now ready to fight.

"How do I know?" Hi asked.

"If I thought you meant that———-"

"Well?" asked Hi Martin, gazing coolly into the flashing eyes.

"You know better!" choked Teall.

"Of course you know better, Hi Martin," Dick broke in. "Ted Teall isn't any more of a thief than you are."

"You fellows have no share in this matter," Hi retorted coldly. "I'll thank you to keep out, and to mind your own business."

A little way down the street Hi caught sight of his father approaching. He turned to Ted to inquire:

"You say that you looked faithfully for my watch until dark?"

"Yes; I did," Ted shot back at him.

"And you didn't find the watch?"

"No, sirree; I didn't."

"Oh, well, then," drawled Hi, "I guess———-"

Grinning broadly, he thrust a hand in under his clothing, drawing out his gold watch.

"I guess," Hi continued, "that it's time now to quit looking. It's quarter of nine. Good night!"

At sight of that watch Ted Teall's eyes bulged. Then the nature of the outrage dawned on him. In a moment all his pent-up emotions took the form of intense indignation.

"You mean fellow!" hissed Ted, his fists clenching. "You———-"

"Teall, when you play jokes," warned Martin coolly, "you always want to be sure to look out for the flare-back. Don't forget that. Good evening, father!"

Hi slipped off by the side of his parent just in time for Ted to slow down and realize that he couldn't very well thrash Hi with the elder Martin looking on. Tom and Greg began to laugh.

"Oh, cheer up, Ted," Dick smiled. "All's well that ends well, you know."

"But this matter isn't ended yet," cried Ted Teall excitedly, shaking his fist at Hi Martin's receding back. "It isn't ended—-no, sir!—-not by a long shot!"

Chapter XII

Nor was Teall long in finding his opportunity to be revenged.

On the following Tuesday, immediately after school, the North and South Grammar nines met on the field. It was an important meeting, for, under the rules governing the Gridley Grammar League, whichever of these two teams lost, having been twice defeated, was to retire vanquished; the victor in this game was to meet the Central Grammar to contest for the championship.

On the toss Captain Ted Teall won, and elected that his side go to bat forthwith.

The instant that Ted stepped to the plate a score of North Grammar fans yelled:

"Bang!"

From another group of Norths came:

"Ow-ow-ow!" This was followed by some fantastic jumping.

"Huh! Those fellows don't show much brains!" uttered Teall wearily. "They have to steal a josh from the Centrals."

It did not annoy Ted to-day. He had expected this greeting, and had steeled himself against it.

Dick & Co., with a lot of other fellows from Central Grammar, looked on in amusement.

"It's a pity one of Hi's fellows hasn't ingenuity enough to work up a new 'gag,'" Tom remarked dryly.

"They'll never rattle Teall again with a 'bang,'" smiled Prescott.

When the Souths went to grass, however, and the Norths took to the benches, all was in readiness for Hi, who came forth third on the batting list. The first two men had been struck out.

"Come on in!" yelled a dozen tormentors from South Grammar onlookers. "The water's fine!"

In spite of himself Hi frowned. He had been expecting something, but had hoped that the events of the preceding Saturday afternoon would be left out.

Hi made a swing for the ball, and missed.

73

"Who's seen my duds?" went up a mighty shout.

"Confound the hoodlums!" hissed Martin between his teeth.

As mascot, the Souths had brought along a small colored boy, who attended to a pail of lemonade for the refreshment of Ted's players. Ere the ball came over the plate a second time this mascot was seen running close to the foul lines. Over one arm he carried jacket and trousers; in the other hand he bore a pair of shoes and of socks. That the clothing was patched and the shoes looked fit only for a tramp's use did not disguise the meaning of the scene from any beholder, for the news of that Saturday afternoon had traveled through the school world of Gridley.

"Cheer up, suh!" shrieked the colored boy shrilly. "I'se bringing yo' duds!"

Then the ball came from the box, but Hi was demoralized by the roar of laughter that swept over the field.

A moment later the rather haughty captain of the North Grammar nine had been struck out and retired. His face was red, his eyes flashing.

"Teall, we might expect something rowdyish from your crowd of muckers," declared Martin scornfully, as the sides changed.

"If I were you, Martin, I wouldn't do much talking to-day," grinned Ted. "It's bad for the nerves."

A half a dozen times thereafter the colored boy was seen scurrying with "the duds." He took good care, however, to keep away from the foul lines, and so did not come under the orders of the umpire.

Whenever the mascot appeared with his burden he raised a laugh. Hi could not steel himself against a combination of anger and hurt pride. Some of the North Grammar girls in whose eyes he was anxious to stand well were among those who could not help laughing at the ridiculous antics of the colored lad.

Toward the close of the first half of the third inning Teall again came to bat. There were no men out in this inning, and two men were on bases.

"Now we'll see how you will stand a little jogging," muttered Hi under his breath as he crossed his hands in signal to some of the North Grammar fans.

Just as Ted picked up his bat a dozen boys squeaked:

"What time is it?"

This was followed by:

"Who stole my watch?"

Another lot of North tormentors——those who had them——displayed time pieces.

"That's almost as bad as a stale one," Ted told himself scornfully.

Just then the ball came just where Teall wanted it.

Crack! Ted hit it a resounding blow, dropped his bat and started to run. Amid a din of yells one of the Souths came in, another reached third and Ted himself rested safely at second base.

In that inning the Souths piled up five runs. Thereafter the game went badly for the North Grammars, for most of the players lost their nerve. Hi, himself, proved unworthy to be captain, he had so little head left for the game. The contest ended with a score of nine to two in favor of the South Grammars.

"That will be about all for the Norths," remarked Ted, with a cheerful grin, as be met Hi Martin at the close of the game. "Your nine doesn't play any more, I believe."

"I'm glad we don't," choked Hi. "There's no satisfaction being in a league in which the other teams are made up of rowdies."

"It is tough," mocked Ted. "Especially when the rowdies are the only fellows who know how to play ball."

Hi stalked away in moody, but dignified silence. Yet, though he could ignore the players and sympathizers of other nines, it was not so easy to get away from the grilling of his own schoolmates.

"Huh!" remarked one North boy. "You told us, Martin, that you'd prove to us the benefit of having a real captain for a nine. Why didn't you?"

"Martin, you're all wind," growled another keenly disappointed North. "You talked a lot about what you'd do with the nine——and what have you done? Left us the boobies of the league. We're the winners of the leather medal."

"Why didn't you play yourself, then?" snarled Hi.

"I wish I had. But we Norths were fooled by the talk you gave us about how baseball really ought to be played and managed. You're the school's mascot, you are, Hi Martin. Not!"

In the meantime Dick Prescott was being surrounded by anxious Central Grammar boys.

"Dick," said one of them, while others listened eagerly, "you beat the Norths. But you didn't give them any such drubbing as the Souths did to-day. Are they a better nine than ours?"

"No," Prescott answered promptly.

"Yet they whipped the Norths worse than we did. Can we down the Souths?"

"Yes," nodded Prescott.

"Why can we?"

"For the simplest reason in the world, Tolman. We've got to. Isn't that a fine reason?"

"It sounds fine," remarked another boy doubtfully. "But can you whip another crowd just because you want to?"

"If you want to badly enough," Dick smiled.

"Hm! I'll be surer about that when I see it done."

"It'll happen next Friday afternoon, if rain doesn't call the game," Prescott promised.

"What do you say to that, Darrin?" demanded another Central boy.

"Just what Dick said."

"What's your word, Tom!"

"You heard what our captain said," Reade laughed. "I always follow orders. If Dick Prescott tells me to pile up seven runs against the Souths I'm going to do it."

"I hope you do," murmured another boy. "Yet it seems against us——after the way we saw the Souths play to-day."

"Or rather," added Dick quietly, "the way the North Grammars didn't play. They'd have put up a lot better game if their captain hadn't lost his nerve and his head."

As the Central Grammar boys left, most of them in one crowd, there was a rather general feeling that Dick was just a bit too confident. Or, was he simply "putting it on," in order to bolster up the courage of his players?

Dick Prescott, at least, was qualified to know what he really expected. He really was confident of victory in the game that should decide the league championship.

"If you feel that you can't be beaten, and won't be beaten, but that you've got to win and are going to win, then that's more than half the points of a game won in advance," he told his chums. "Fellows, in baseball or anything else, we won't say die, either now or at any later time in life. We'll make it our rule to ride right over anything that gets in our way. That way we can't know defeat."

"Unless, finally, we ride to our deaths," laughed Tom.

"What of it?" challenged Dick. "That wouldn't be defeat. The man who rides to death in the search for victory has won. He has carried the winning spirit with him to the very finish. Or else the history we've been studying at school is all a mess of lies."

"There's a lot in that idea," nodded Dave thoughtfully.

"There's more in it every time that you think of it," Dick contended.

Thus Dick was starting, in Dick & Co., the never-give-up spirit which made them almost invincible later as High School boys.

Wednesday and Thursday were days filled with eagerness for the Central Grammar boys. The members of the baseball squad were not by any means the only ones on tenterhooks. Every boy in the upper grades of the school was waiting impatiently to learn who would be the winners of the championship.

Somewhat to the astonishment of the Central Grammar boys Captain Dick, on Wednesday afternoon, gave his team only a brief half hour of diamond practice. Thursday afternoon they didn't play at all. Instead, the nine and its subs. went off on a tramp through the woods.

"What we want to-morrow above all," Dick explained, as he marshaled his forces, "is steady nerves. There's nothing like a good walk in the cool and shady spots for tuning up a schoolboy's nerves for an ordeal. A walk is good whether you're facing an exam. or a championship game."

"May the rest of us go with you!" called one of the Central boys outside the squad.

"We can't stop you," Dick replied, "but we'd rather you let the ball squad go by itself."

"All right, then," cried three or four. The fourteen of the squad marched away, unhampered by any followers.

Once outside the town and halted under a grove of trees, Dick turned to his teammates.

"Fellows," he said quietly, "I believe some of you have been anxious to know what the man on the clubhouse steps said."

"It's coming, at last!" gasped Tom Reade. "Well, let us hear what the man on the clubhouse steps said. It must be one of the choice pieces of wisdom of all the ages."

"It is," Dick replied quietly.

"Then let us hear shouted Dave.

"Not now," Prescott answered, shaking his head solemnly. "But, fellows, you win to-morrow's game and you shall all hear just what the man on the clubhouse steps said."

"Win?" retorted Tom Reade. "Dick Prescott, with a bribe like that before us, we're bound to win! We couldn't do anything else."

Then they went further into the woods. Dick had brought his players here in search of peace, quiet and nerve rest. Had he had even one prophetic glimpse of what was ahead of some of them that afternoon it would have been far better to have remained in town.

Chapter XIII

"BIG INJUN—-HEAP BIG NOISE"

"Say, we don't want to just go on walking. There's no fun in that," objected Spoff Henderson.

"We're out for rest more than for fun," Dick replied. "The walk and the rest this afternoon are all by way of preparing for the big game to-morrow afternoon."

"But wouldn't there be more rest about it if we had a little fun?" Spoff insisted.

"Perhaps," Dick nodded. "What's your idea of fun?"

"Why not play 'Indians and Whites'?" put in Toby Ross eagerly.

"That would be just the sort of game for to-day," Dave approved.

"That's what I say," nodded Tom.

"Dick, you're used to these woods," Spoff went on. "You be the big Injun—- the big chief. Choose two more of the fellows to be Injuns with you, and the rest will be whites."

"All right," nodded Dick. "Dave and Tom can go with me. Who'll be your captain?"

"Greg!" cried Spoff.

"Holmesy," said Ross in the same breath.

So Greg Holmes was chosen captain, to command the whites.

"Give us the full six minutes, Greg, won't you?" Dick called, as he and his two fellow "Injuns" prepared to enter the deep woods.

"Of course I will," Greg nodded. "You don't think I'd cheat, do you?"

Those of the boys who were proud owners of watches hurriedly consulted their timepieces. Greg retained his in his hand.

"Now," called Dick, and away he started, followed by Braves Darrin and Reade.

As the Gridley boys had their own version of "Indians and Whites," a description of the game may as well be given here.

The Indians always chose a chief, the whites a captain. Chief and braves

79

started away at the call of time. Six minutes later, to the second, the whites started in pursuit. The whites must keep in one band, as must also the Indians. Yet, in trailing, the whites could spread out, while the Indians must keep together.

Though the Indians were allowed to double on the trail, they were not permitted to run. Nothing faster than an ordinary walk was permitted to them, unless they found themselves sighted by the whites.

Moreover, owing to the lack of skill on the part of the whites in following a trail, the Indians were required to walk as usual, making no special efforts to hide their footprints.

The whites were permitted to pursue at any gait. If they sighted the Indians, then they were expected to yell by way of warning. If more than half the Indians were captured before the expiration of an hour from the first departure of the Indians, then the whites won. Otherwise the Indians were victors.

Dick walked in advance, Dave and Tom side by side just behind him.

"We must try to think up some way to fool the fellows," muttered Reade.

"Halt!" warned Dick, when they were barely two minutes away from the starting point.

Darrin and Reade stopped in their tracks.

"See that low-hanging limb, and the bushes just beyond?" asked young Prescott.

"Of course," assented Dave.

"We'll go on about a minute further," suggested Dick, who had kept his watch in hand from the outset. "Then we'll walk backward, stop here, grab that limb and swing ourselves over past the bushes. That ought to throw the fellows off the track and get 'em all mixed up."

"If the whites are spread enough they'll probably be outside those bushes," remarked Reade. "Then they'll find where the trail changes."

"That's one of the chances that we have to take," smiled Dick.
"Let's see if we can't make it work."

Onward again they went, halting when Prescott gave the word. Walking backward, they were soon at the oak with the low-hanging limb.

"I'll try it first," proposed Dick, "and see if it's easy enough. Don't walk around here and make enough tracks to call the attention of the whites to the fact that we stopped here."

Dick made a bound, catching the limb fairly. Three or four times he swung himself back and forth, until he had gained enough momentum. Then he let go, on the last swing, landing on his feet well behind the bushes. Dave came next, Tom following. Now the three Indians hurried on again, Big Injun Dick in the lead as before.

"If we do throw them off, Greg's fighting men will have a hard job hitting the trail again," chuckled Tom.

"If they don't find our trail, Dick, where are you headed for?" whispered Dave.

"For the road and home," laughed Dick. "Then, while they're trying to figure out where we've gone, we fellows will be washing up for supper."

"I'd like to hear Old Greg grumbling if the 'double' does throw 'em off the trail altogether," grinned Darrin. "Dick, I think we've more than half a chance to get away."

"We have about four chances out of five of slipping away from Greg's soldiers," predicted Prescott.

For ten minutes Dick and his two braves plodded on. There were, as yet, no audible sounds of pursuit.

"We caught 'em, surely enough, that time," chuckled Tom. "Going to hit for the road now, Dick?"

"We can't reach the road until our hour is up; we're bound to keep to the woods," Prescott replied. "However, you'll note that I am taking a course that will gradually lead us to the road."

"Right-o," nodded Reade, after taking a look at their surroundings. All the members of Dick & Co. had spent so much of their time in the woods that they knew every foot of the way.

"I wonder where that valiant band of whites is, anyway?" muttered Dave. "I haven't heard a sound of them."

"You may hear their battle yell any minute," Dick whispered. "Be careful not to talk loudly enough to give them any clue."

For two or three minutes more Dick led the way. Of a sudden he halted—right up against a huge surprise. For the boys had suddenly broken into a little circular clearing, not much more than thirty feet in diameter. Near the center of this clearing, under a flimsy shelter he had made of poles and branches, crouched Amos Garwood. He was at work over a low bench built of a board across two boxes. So intent was Garwood on what he was doing that he appeared not to have heard the approach of the boys.

Dick Prescott stood looking on, one hand raised as a signal for the silence of those behind him. But both Dave and Tom had caught sight of the stranger at about the same instant.

"If any who know me have hinted that my brain is not strong enough," muttered Garwood, whose back was turned to the startled Grammar School boys, "there is bound to be a great awakening when my wonderful invention is perfected. Then the world will bow down to me, for I shall be its master."

"Crazy as a porous plaster!" muttered Tom Reade under his breath.

"It will be a new, a strange sensation," continued Garwood, speaking just loud enough to be heard by the onlookers. "A great sensation, too, to be master of the world when, during these present dark days, I am compelled to run and hide for fear envious scientists will succeed in capturing me and locking me up."

"I wonder what he thinks he's doing there?" pondered Dick curiously.

"To think that a few grains of this wonderful substance would pulverize a regiment!" continued Garwood, in an inventor's ecstasy. "An ounce of this wonderful material enough to blow up an army corps. A single pound sufficient to bring the nations of the world to my feet in awed homage. And I can make a hundred pounds a day of it! Oh, that I could reach other worlds, to make them feel my mastery!"

"If his stuff is as good as he thinks it is, I certainly hope he won't shoot off any of it accidentally," thought Prescott, with an odd little shiver.

"Oh, that I dared trust my secret to one or two others!" murmured Garwood, as he delved with one hand into one of the boxes that supported his simple bench. "And now for the great finishing touch!"

Amos Garwood placed on the board a fairsized wide-mouthed bottle. From where he stood, Dick could read the label on the bottle—- "Potassium Chlorate—-crystals."

"Chlorate of potash?" thought Dick. "That's what Dr. Bentley gave me once for sore throat."

Dick, however, was soon to get an inkling of a suspicion that chlorate of potash might be used to serve other purposes.

As the mentally queer inventor reached into the box for that bottle, the three silent, observing "Injuns" saw that Garwood had on the crude table before him a glass mortar and pestle, the former of about two quarts' capacity.

In this mortar lay a quantity of powdered stuff, which Garwood had evidently been grinding before their arrival. Now he poured out a heaping handful of the chlorate crystals, dropping them on top of the mixture in the mortar.

"A few turns——a little more fatigue of the wrist——and I am the world's master——its owner!" cried Garwood exultantly.

"Ker-choo!" sneezed Tom Reade at the worst possible moment.

Amos Garwood turned like a flash, tottering to his feet.

"Spies! Traitors! Ingrates!" he gasped in hoarse terror.

"Nothing at all like it," Dick replied, with a pleasant smile. "Mr. Garwood, we boys are playing in these woods. If we've meddled with your affairs you'll pardon us, and let us pass on, won't you?"

"Didn't you try to find me here?" demanded Garwood, suspicious still.

"I give you my word of honor that we didn't, sir," answered Dick. "Until a moment ago we hadn't any idea that you were within fifty miles of this spot. You see, sir, we're playing Indians and whites. We're the big Injuns, even if we don't look it. And behind us, somewhere on our trail, is Captain Greg Holmes, with a company of his brave soldiers, trailing us relentlessly."

"Soldiers?" quivered Amos Garwood, his face going ashen. Then his face suddenly took on a look of intense exultation. "Soldiers?" he repeated. "It couldn't be better. It is on soldiers that my amazing discovery should be proved. But I waste time——and loss of time may be fatal to all my plans. A few turns, and my discovery is ready. I can then defy whole armies, if necessary!"

Sweeping the mortar around within reach, so that he could work and watch the Grammar School boys at the same time, Amos Garwood began to grind his pestle into the mixture with feverish energy.

Then all of a sudden the very earth shook and rocked. Big Injun Prescott and his two braves were in the center of the biggest explosion they had ever heard!

Chapter XIV

It was terrific, and yet the only effect on the bench on which the mortar lay was to knock the board sideways from the boxes. The mortar became as powder itself, though not a splinter was raised from the wood.

From the lips of Amos Garwood a fearful yell went up. He plunged headlong a few feet, then lay on the ground, feebly nursing his right hand with his left.

As for Dick, Dave and Tom, their ears rang with the noise until they felt as though surely their ear-drums had been ruptured by the force of that awesome detonation.

An instant later all was quiet. Dick and his chums speedily realized that they had escaped actual injury, yet their legs shook so that they could hardly stand.

"Wh—-wh—-what was it?" asked Reade in accents that quivered in unison with his trembling legs.

"See here, fellows, we mustn't be fools," Dick cried chidingly. "We're not hurt, and Mr. Garwood is. Let's see what we can do for him."

"Do for me, will you?" groaned the injured one. "No, you won't. You boys keep your distance from me, or you're going to be worse scared than you are already. Don't imagine that I'm helpless, for I'm not. In me you behold the master of the world!"

"Confound him, I've a good mind to go away and let him have the world to himself," muttered Reade.

But Dick and Dave had already started toward the spot where Amos lay. The man scrambled to his feet, the old, hunted look coming into his eyes.

"You keep away from me!" he screamed. "Get away! Clear out! I don't want to hurt you. I wouldn't harm a fly. But I'm not going to allow any one near me!"

Dick ventured too near. Garwood swung his uninjured arm so unexpectedly that Prescott had no chance to get out of the way. He fell flat on the ground. Warned by the light in the eye of the world's master, Dick believed it prudent to roll several yards before be tried to get up.

"Say," blazed Darrin indignantly. "Are you going to stand for that?"

"Don't excite him," murmured Prescott in an undertone. "The poor fellow isn't responsible for what he's doing. And I'd fight, too, if I thought any one was trying to seize me."

"I'm sorry if I had to hurt you," said Amos Garwood in a milder tone. "But I allow no one to come near me. I have too many enemies —-so many who are jealous of me that I can trust no one."

"He isn't really dangerous, poor fellow," whispered Prescott to his companions.

"No, though he has a habit of blowing up suddenly," muttered Reade. "He did the same thing once before, you'll remember, at the old water-works cottage."

"Are we going to try to catch the fellow this time?" Darrin whispered.

"Yes," nodded Dick. "We ought to, both for his father's sake and his own."

"What do you say, then, if we all three rush him?" pressed Darrin.

"It would be mean," Dick retorted in an undertone. "The poor fellow might be tempted to use his injured hand. And you can see how it's burned. I don't wonder. You saw how the flame of the explosion leaped all over that arm. It's a wonder it didn't set him afire."

"Are you boys going to leave me," inquired Garwood, "or are you going to remain and thus show me that you are truly of my enemies?"

"You slip back into the woods, Tom," whispered Dick. "See if you can find Greg and the other fellows. If you can, bring them up quickly."

Dave and I'll stay here, unless Garwood moves away. If he does, Darry and I will follow him. If you hear any war whoops, come running in that direction, you and the other fellows. You'll know that the whoop means that we need you."

"I hate to leave you two with him," muttered Reade reluctantly. "If this world-boss gets violent you two won't be enough for him."

"We can get out of the way, if we have to," Dick rejoined. "But hurry, Tom. We need a lot of the fellows, for we ought to seize this poor fellow and get him into town, even if only that he may have proper attention for his burned hand and arm. Hustle. You'll help me more in that way than in any other."

Thus urged, Tom turned and vanished into the forest behind the others.

"Why do you stay here?" demanded Amos Garwood fretfully. "I don't want to injure you, boys; but if you belong to my enemies, then I shall be forced to hurt you. Run away before I lose my temper. I am always sorry afterwards when I have lost my temper."

The flash in the man's eyes made both boys feel "creepy." Thin as he was, there was about him, none the less, a suggestion of great strength and force when put in action.

"We have a right to stay in the woods, Mr. Garwood," Dick answered. "I don't want to seem impudent, either, but I would suggest that if you don't like to be with us here, then there are other parts of the forest that you can find."

As Dick spoke he swung one arm, pointing artfully to the woods in the direction that Tom Reade had gone, and where it was believed that Greg and his followers were searching.

"If that's the way you want me to go," smiled Amos Garwood darkly, "then I believe I'll go in the opposite direction. And, young men, it won't be wise for you to attempt to follow me!"

With that hint he started. Dick and Dave waited until they could see only the top of his head. Then they started on his trail.

For an instant Amos Garwood was out of sight. Then, with a suddenness that startled both trailers, Garwood stepped out from behind a tree and right into their path.

"I cautioned you both," he announced sharply. "I shall not go to that trouble again. Keep away from me. Never mind where I am going, or what I am going to do."

Then a spasm of pain shot across the poor fellow's face. Calm as he tried to keep himself, it was plain that his burned hand and arm were causing him great suffering.

"Won't you come with us," pleaded Dick, "and get that arm of yours attended to? We'll take you to the right place."

"To the right place?" mocked Garwood harshly. "Right into the camp of my enemies, I suppose? Among those who deride my great invention, and yet who would capture me and steal my wonderful discovery from me. Boys, I have already told you that if you follow me, you will follow me to grave harm. Beware in time. Run! Leave me! Or your fates be on your own heads, for I am master of the world and can force you to obey me!"

As Garwood spoke the last words another change crossed his face.
He reached into an inner coat pocket.

"You will not obey me," he remarked. "Therefore, I must act to save myself and my great discovery. 'Tis as you would have it!"

"Duck!" gasped Dave Darrin, seizing Dick by one arm. "He means big mischief!"

What it was for which he had reached in his pocket neither Grammar School boy saw, for both turned at the same instant, beating a swift retreat. Sixty feet away, however, they halted, wheeling about.

Garwood, seeing the boys run, acted as though he would give them no further thought. He was already walking in the opposite direction, his back turned to them.

"Ugh! He gives me cold chills," cried Darrin.

"He does the same to me," sighed Dick, "but it's a plain case of duty to follow him until we can turn him over to those who'll take good care of the poor fellow."

Just as Amos Garwood was on the point of vanishing from their view, the two schoolboys started forward, more cautiously than before.

Back of them in the woods, far away, sounded a boyish war-whoop.

"Hi-yi-yi-yi-*yoop!*" answered Dave Darrin.

Amos Garwood started forward with a bound like that of a deer. Then his long legs went into rapid operation. Prescott and Darrin ran onward as fast as they could go. They were trained to running, too, but this "master of the world" set them a pace that no fourteen-year-old boys on earth could have followed with any hope of success.

"Whoop, but he's an airship for speed!" gasped Dave Darrin.

"We couldn't catch him with a locomotive," confessed Dick, when, panting, he was at last obliged to halt.

"Hear him——going," gasped Darrin.

"I can't hear him," confessed Dick, after a moment of listening.

"That's just the point. He has gotten so far away that we can't hear him crashing through the undergrowth."

"I'm afraid we won't catch up with him again to-day," sighed Dick.

"The folks who are trying to catch Amos Garwood are foolish in sending detectives to look for him," muttered Dave. "They ought to hire professional sprinters."

Away at their rear sounded a fainter whoop.

"Answer the fellows, Dave," urged Prescott.

"I will——when I get some wind," muttered Darrin.

Three times more Greg and his fellows whooped before Dick could get together enough wind to make his voice travel. Greg repeated the hail, and again Dick answered. After a few minutes the other Grammar School boys caught up with Dick and his friend, who told to the new-comers the story of the encounter with Amos Garwood.

"Get away from you again?" asked Tom blankly.

"I don't believe we'll ever chase that streak of light again," growled Dave. "I don't feel as though I'd ever be able to run again. Amos Garwood can walk faster than any of us can run."

"The most that we can do at present," Prescott concluded, will be to notify Lawyer Ripley or Chief Coy that we've seen the Garwood flyer again."

"I wish we could catch him," sighed Torn, while Greg nodded.

"You two can have the next chance," smiled Dick. "As for me, I am certain that I can never catch Amos Garwood unless he and I happen to be running toward each other."

"All in favor of supper," proposed Dan Dalzell, glancing at his watch, "say 'aye' and turn homeward."

"But shan't we try, for a while, to trail Garwood?" queried Greg.

"What's the use?" cross-questioned Dick disconsolately. "We might sight him, but we'd never catch him. Nor do I believe he has stopped running yet."

"If he hasn't," grumbled Dave, "he's twenty miles from here by this time."

So Dan's motion prevailed. The baseball squad of the Central Grammar School turned toward the road that led homeward.

Chapter XV

"That explosion was fearful, what there was of it," Dick declared to Chief Coy. It was evening, and the head of the local police department had stopped the boys on the street for additional information on the subject.

"What did it look like?" asked Chief Coy.

"There came a big flash and a loud bang in the same instant, and Mr. Garwood was hurled over on his side. The queer part of it was that the explosion didn't do any real damage to the bench, though there wasn't a piece of the glass mortar left that was big enough to see."

"The explosion all went upward. It didn't work sideways or downward?" asked Chief Coy.

"That's the way we saw it," Dick replied. "And it didn't hurt either you or Darrin?"

"Not beyond the big scare, and the shock to our ear-drums."

"I wonder what the explosive could have been?" mused the chief aloud.

"I don't know what was in the mortar in the first place, sir," Dick Prescott went on. "All Amos Garwood put in the mortar after we got there was some chlorate of potash. Then he put the pestle in and began to grind."

"And then the explosion happened?" followed up Chief Coy.

"Chlorate of potash, eh?" broke in a local druggist, who had halted and was listening. "Hm! If Garwood ground that stuff with a pestle, then it doesn't much matter what else was in the mortar!"

"Is the chlorate explosive, sir?" questioned Dick.

"Is it?" mimicked the druggist. "When I first started in to learn the drug business it was a favorite trick to give an apprentice one or two small crystals of chlorate to grind in a mortar. After a lot of accidents, and after a few drug clerks had been send to jail for playing the trick it became played out in drug stores."

"But I've seen powdered chlorate of potash," interposed Tom Reade, who was always in search of information.

"Yes," admitted the druggist. "I can show you, at my store, about ten pounds of the powdered chlorate."

"Then how do they get it into a powder, sir?" pressed Tom. "Do the manufacturers grind it between big millstones?"

"If any ever did," laughed the druggist, "they never remained on earth long enough to tell about it. A few pounds of the chlorate, crushed between millstones, would blow the roof off of the largest mill you ever saw!"

"But what makes the stuff so explosive?" queried Prescott.

"I don't know whether I can make you understand it," the druggist replied. "Potassium chlorate is extremely 'rich' in oxygen, and it is held very loosely in combination. When a piece of the chlorate is struck a hard blow it sets the oxygen free, and the gas expands so rapidly that the explosion follows."

On the outskirts of the little crowd stood a new-comer, Ted Teall, who was drinking in every word that the druggist uttered. Dick saw him and felt a sudden start of intuition.

"See here, Teall," Dick called, "you needn't pick that up as a pointer for the way to serve me with a home-made ball at our game to-morrow. The trick I played on you wasn't dangerous, but this chlorate racket is. Mr. Johnson, what would happen if a fellow should hit a ball with his bat, and that ball was packed with chlorate of potash?"

"I'm not sure that the fellow with the bat would ever know what happened," answered the druggist.

"Is it as bad as that?" gasped Teall.

"Worse," replied the druggist grimly.

"So, Teall, if you had any thoughts of playing a trick like that," interposed Chief Coy, "take my word for it that such a trick would be likely to land you in a reform school until you were at least twenty-one years old."

"Oh, if it's as bad as that——-" muttered Ted reluctantly.

"What did you and Darry say, when the explosion came off?" asked Dan Dalzell, as Dick & Co. walked on again.

"I don't remember just what Darry said," Prescott confessed reluctantly. "As for me, I remember just what I said."

"What?"

"I said just what the man on the clubhouse steps said."

"And what was that?" pressed Dalzell.

"That's what you're going to find out if you win the game from South Grammar to-morrow."

"Then the game is as good as won already," declared Tom solemnly, "for we're in that frame of mind where we've got to know what the man on the clubhouse steps said."

Through the evening, and the long night that followed, Chief Coy had two of his policemen out searching the woods where Garwood had last been seen. Mr. Winthrop added three detectives to the chase. When morning came the "queer" inventor was still at large. He had not even been seen since Dick and Dave had lost sight of him.

"The last time that I put this class on honor," announced Old Put, when the morning session began, "we had one of the best records of good behavior during the day that I can remember. I will, therefore, announce that this class is on honor again to-day, and that, no matter what the breaches of discipline, no pupil will be kept after school to-day. All will be allowed to go and see the great, the glorious game."

Then, after a pause, Old Dut added dryly:

"I haven't the heart to keep any one after school to-day. I am going to the game myself."

At this statement a laugh rippled around the room. Then every boy and girl settled down to the serious business of the day.

At three o'clock Old Put announced:

"If Captain Prescott so desires, he may withdraw now with his team, in order to have time to dress and get oiled up on the diamond."

"I thank you, sir, for that permission," responded Dick, rising at once. He was followed by the other players.

"Go out a little more quietly, if you please——that's all," called Old Dut.

On tiptoe the members of the squad stole upstairs to the exhibition hall. There they quickly got into their uniforms, next stowing their street clothing in a closet, the key of which the principal had supplied to Captain Dick Prescott.

In thoughtful silence Dick led his small host from the schoolhouse to the diamond. When they had halted by the benches Dick began:

"Now, fellows, each of you keep steadily in mind what we have at stake this afternoon."

"Yes, sirree!" grinned Dan Dalzell. "If we win to-day we're going to learn what the man on the clubhouse steps said."

"To-day's victory gives one school or the other the championship of the Gridley Grammar School League," Dick declared.

"Oh, that's a side issue, entirely," retorted Tom gravely. "What we're really burning about is to know what the man on the clubhouse steps said."

"Are we going to pitch in to practice now?" asked Greg.

"You fellows can, if you want to, but don't go at it too hard," replied Captain Dick.

"If you didn't want to practice, what were you in such a hurry to get out of school for?" demanded Holmes.

"Because I felt that we had been in school about as long as we could stand on the day of the championship game," laughed Prescott.

"Wise captain," approved Darrin.

They had not been on the field many minutes when a whoop sounded near at hand that caused the boys to look with surprise.

"Here come the Souths!" called Dave. "They must have been let out early, too."

"Hello!" hailed Captain Teall. "You fellows are here early, but
I don't see your shovels."

"Shovels?" repeated Dick.

"Yes; to dig holes to get into after the game is over," Ted retorted.

"Teall," Prescott responded sternly, "if the South Grammars want any holes to hide in, they'll have to dig them themselves."

"Humph! We'll see which side feels most like digging a hole when the score is read!" retorted Ted. "Come along, Souths!"

Ted led the way down the field for practice. On the way he turned to shout something back. At that moment he tripped over a small wooden box and fell flat.

"Oh, Ted!" called Dick hurriedly.

"Well?" growled Teall, rubbing his shins.

"Did you enjoy your little trip?"

"My—-little—-trip?" repeated Ted wonderingly. "Oh—-pshaw!
Of course you'd think of something like that to say."

"If you're lamed any by your little trip," offered Tom, "I'll leave left field to do your base running for you this afternoon."

"Yah! I'll bet you would," jeered Teall. "And if I let you, I'd be down on the score card for three less than no runs at all."

"You will, anyway," said Reade gravely.

"Somehow," broke in Dan, "I feel unusually happy this afternoon."

"That's because you know we're going to win to-day," laughed Dick.

"Oh, that's a part of it, yes," Dalzell agreed. "But the real cause of my happy feeling is that I'm going to find out what the man on the clubhouse steps said. That's what I've been aching to know ever since some time last winter."

"The time will pass shortly now, Danny Grin," Prescott remarked comfortingly.

By this time a score of spectators had arrived. Then came a few High School boys, among them Ben Tozier, who was again to umpire. "Tozier, what's the High School delegation for?" Dan asked. "To find out who'll be handy for the High School nine next year?"

"Perhaps," Ben replied gravely. "There's some good, young material in the two nines, all right. The trouble is that a lot of you fellows won't go to High School."

"All of Dick & Co. are going to attend High School," Dave proudly informed Tozier.

Two more High School boys now appeared who were not as welcome. Fred Ripley and Bert Dodge walked on to the field side by side.

"What are they doing here?" asked Dave.

"We are in luck," spoke up Tom, "if they haven't come here to start mischief."

"If they do, if they even try it," Dick predicted grimly, "they'll be the ones out of luck. We'll turn the boys of two Grammar Schools loose on them and run them off the field."

Down the street sounded a noise that could come from only one cause. Central Grammar School had "let out." All the boys and many of the girls were now hurrying toward the ball field. It was natural to take the biggest sort of interest in this game, which was to decide which school was the "champion."

"I'm sorry to see your crowd in such high spirits, Prescott," said Ted Teall, coming up. "It'll be all the harder for Central Grammar to bear when the score

93

is announced."

"You're sure of winning, then, Teall?" Dick inquired.

"Absolutely certain!" Captain Ted rejoined.

"We're going to set off a big bonfire this evening, Ted," Captain Prescott rejoined. "If we win to-day will you agree to be on hand to light the fire?"

"Yes; if you win," agreed Ted. "But you can't!"

Chapter XVI

The umpire's quiet voice called the captains of the nines apart.

"Who'll call the toss?" asked Ben.

"Let Teall do it," Dick answered.

"You do it, Prescott," urged Captain Ted.

"Well, which one of you is going to call?" inquired Tozier.

"Teall," Dick again answered.

"Oh, all right, then," nodded Ted. "I suppose, Prescott, you feel that, whichever way I call, I'd wish I'd taken the other way."

The coin spun upward in the air, for Ben Tozier was a master of the art of flipping.

"Tails," announced Teall.

"It's heads this time," announced Umpire Tozier. "Captain Prescott?"

"We'll go to bat, then," decided Prescott. "We might as well begin to pile up the score that we're going to make."

"We'll show you how you're not going to make it," Ted grinned. "Remember, Prescott, that I and Wells are the battery to-day."

"What you need," laughed Dick, "is a good right fielder and a star third baseman."

"Huh!" grunted Teall.

"Get to your places," ordered Tozier briskly. "We want to end this game some time to-day."

The umpire inspected a new ball, then sent it grounding to Teall. Back and forth between the members of the South Grammar battery the ball passed three times.

"Play ball!" called the umpire sharply.

Tom Reade already stood by the plate. He swung his stick idly, watching Teall. Along came the ball. Tom judged it and hit at it.

"Strike one!" called Tozier, shifting a pebble to his left hand.

Ted grinned derisively as he twisted the leather for the next throw.

"Ball one!" and a bean followed the pebble into the umpire's left hand.

"Strike two! Ball two! Ball three!"

Ted Teall began to feel angry over the growing pile of called balls. He delivered one with great care.

Whack! Tom never waited to see whether the ball was headed inside or outside of foul lines. He simply dropped his willow, then gave his best exhibition of the sprinting that he had learned in the spring.

It was a fair ball that struck inside of left field. South's left fielder had to run in for the leather, which struck the ground, then rolled to one side. Thump! The ball landed neatly in the first baseman's hands, but Tom had kicked the bag a second before.

"Runner safe," drawled Tozier.

Spoff Henderson came next to bat. Ted, with great care, struck him out. Toby Ross met with similar disaster, nor did Reade have any chance to steal up to second. Then Greg advanced to the plate. He had his own favorite stick, which he swung with great confidence.

"Now, just see what I'll do to you!" was what Ted Teall's impudent smile meant.

Crack! Holmes hit the first ball, reaching first and pushing Tom to second.

"Danny Grin, don't fail us," begged Prescott, as Dan started for the plate. "Two men out, remember!"

As Dalzell faced the pitcher his grin was broader than Teall's.

Two strikes and two balls were quickly called. Some of Dalzell's assurance was gone now, but he steadied himself down. It would never do to strike out at such a time.

Then Danny Grin made his third strike, but he drove the ball ahead of him, forcing the right fielder of the Souths to run backward for it, but he missed the catch and by the time the ball was in circulation again the bases were full of Central Grammar runners.

"I'm glad you're going forward," whispered Dave, just as Dick started towards the plate, his favorite bat in hand.

"I'll make a monkey of you," muttered Teall, just loudly enough for the words to reach Prescott.

"If you can, you're welcome," grunted Dick under his breath.

Swat! It was the first ball driven in. Had there been a fence around the field that fair drive would have gone over it. How it soared and then flew! The right fielder who followed that ball was nervous from the start. He panted as he fell upon the ball.

"Throw it to third!" yelled Teall.

"Just at that instant Dan Dalzell was nearing the home plate, which Tom and Greg had already passed. Prescott's ankle turned slightly or he would have got in ahead of the ball.

"Runner out at third," called Tozier in a singsong voice. "Side out!"

"Yet who cared?" Dick's wonderful blow on the leather had brought three men in safe.

The Souths followed at bat. One, two, three, Prescott struck them out. Ted Teall's face looked solemn, indeed.

"Wells, we've simply got to hold these fellows down," grunted Teall to his catcher in the brief conference for which there was time. "We don't want to be walloped by a score of ninety-four to two."

"I haven't let anything get by me, have I?" grunted the catcher.

"No; but signal for some of my new ones."

"I don't want to put a crimp in your wing," muttered Wells.

"That's all right. It's a tough wing. Don't let the Centrals score anything on us in this inning."

"I'll do my best to help you hold 'em down," promised the South Grammar catcher as he hurried to his place behind the plate.

Dave Darrin, to his intense disgust, was struck out on three of the most crafty throws that Teall had on his list. Hazelton followed. Another player reached first on called balls, but the next Central boy struck a fair, short fly that landed in Ted's own hands.

"That was more like," grunted Ted, as he met his catcher at the bench. "In that first inning these Centrals had me almost scared."

In the second half of this second inning the Souths scored one run. They did the same in the third and the fourth innings, meantime preventing Prescott's fellows from scoring again, though in the fourth inning Prescott saw the bases full with Centrals just before the third man was struck out.

In the fifth and sixth innings neither side scored. At last the spectators began to realize that they were watching two well-matched nines.

"I can't see that the Central Grammars are doing such a lot of a much," grunted Hi Martin to a High School boy.

"The Centrals are playing fine ball," retorted the High School boy. "The only trouble is that the Souths rank pretty close to them."

"I'd like to play both teams again," asserted Hi. "All that happened to us was that we struck a few flukes when we played."

"Humph!" retorted the High School lad, just before turning away. "Your North Grammar nine was kicked all over the field by both of these nines. Both Prescott's and Teall's fellows have improved a lot since they met you."

Hi subsided, feeling unhappy. It hurt him to hear any one praise a fellow like Prescott.

"I wonder if they could beat us, if we had another try?" pondered Hi. "But what's the use of talking? Prescott would never think of giving us another chance. He's too thankful to have lugged the score away from us before."

In the eighth inning Teall brought in one more run for the Souths, who now led.

"We've got to work mighty hard and carefully," grunted Tom Reade.

"Yes," assented Dick briefly.

"We're beaten, anyway, I guess," sighed Hazelton.

Dick Prescott wheeled upon him almost wrathfully.

"We're never beaten, Harry——remember that. We don't propose to be beaten, and we can't be. We're going to bat now to pile up a few more runs. The championship is ours, fellows——don't let that fact escape you."

"I wish I had Dick's confidence," sighed Harry, turning to Reade.

"It isn't confidence; it's nerve," Tom retorted. "If we all show nerve like Dick's, then nothing but the hardest sort of luck can take this game away from us."

Greg went first to bat, securing the first bag. Dick followed, with a two-bagger that brought frantic cheers from the on-looking Central Grammar boys.

"There are our two runs——the ones we need," cheered Darrin to himself, as he snatched up his bat. "Now if I'm any good on earth, I'll bring Greg in and perhaps Dick, too."

Though Dave was excited, he kept the fact to himself, facing Ted Teall with steely composure.

Two strikes and three balls were called. The two base-runners, full of confidence in Darry, were edging off daringly.

"If I dared," throbbed Dave inwardly, "I'd refuse and walk to first on a called ball. But Tozier might call a strike on me——most likely would. Darry, you idiot, you've got to hit the next delivery, even if it goes by you ten feet from the line."

Poising himself on tip-toe, Dave awaited the coming of the ball. Wells, with a wicked grin, signaled for a ball that he felt sure would catch Dave napping. Earlier in the game it might have done so, but Ted's right "wing" was now drooping. Hi did his best, but Dave reached and clubbed the leather. In raced Greg, while Dick had a loafing time on his way to third. Dave reached first in plenty of time.

Two men went out, leaving the nines tied. Dick fumed now at third.

"I wish some one else than Henderson were going to bat," groaned Prescott inwardly.

However, Spoff had the honor of his school desperately at heart. He did his best, watching with cool judgment and backed by an iron determination to make his mark. The third strike he hit. It was enough to bring Prescott in. Dick seemed to travel with the speed of a racing car, reaching the home plate just ahead of the ball.

The side went out right after that.

"What did I tell you?" breathed Dick jubilantly. "We now stand five to four."

"But Ted's terrors have a chance at bat," returned Hazelton.

"It won't do them any good," Captain Dick affirmed. "Greg, signal for all the hard ones. Don't have any mercy on my arm. This is the last inning and the last game of the series. I can stand being crippled."

"The last inning and the last game, unless the Souths score now," Holmes answered.

"Don't *let* 'em score!" Dick insisted. "Remember, kill me with hard work, but don't let the Souths score!"

Ted Teall went to bat first for his side.

Chapter XVII

Teall's grin, as he swung his stick and waited, was more impudent than ever. He meant to show the bumptious Centrals a thing or two.

Then in came Dick's wickedest drop ball, and it looked so good that Captain Ted took a free chance.

"Strike one!" remarked Umpire Tozier.

Some of the grin vanished from Ted's face, but his eyes now flashed the fire of resolve.

"Strike two!"

Teall began to feel little tremors running all up and down his spine.

"Steady, you idiot!" he warned himself.

"Ball one!"

Captain Teall began to feel better. Perhaps Dick's arm was beginning to grow stale.

"Strike three. Out!"

Ted started for the bench, hurling his bat before him. He was full of self-disgust.

"A fellow never can guess when he has Dick thrashed," he said to a South beside him.

"I didn't expect to see you play out before him in the ninth, Ted," replied the classmate.

"Neither did I," muttered Teall gloomily.

"Strike three! Out!" sounded Umpire Tozier's droning voice.

Then Ted sat up straight, rubbing his eyes.

"Two out, and no one on bases!" groaned Ted. "Oh, fellows—-those of you who have a chance—-do something. For goodness' sake, do something to save South Grammar."

A few agonized moments passed while those at the batting benches looked on at the fellow now performing by the plate.

"Strike three! Out!" remarked Ben Tozier decisively. Then the game was given to the Central Grammar boys by a score of five to four. The championship of the local Grammar League was also awarded them.

Ted gulped down hard. Some of his fellows looked decidedly mad.

"It's a shame!" choked Wells.

"No; it isn't, either," Ted disputed. "Dick Prescott and his fellows beat us fairly. Come on we'll congratulate 'em."

Good sportsman that he was, Ted almost limped across the field, followed by some of his players, to where Dick and the other Central Grammar players were surrounded by their friends.

"Prescott, you fellows are wonders!" broke forcefully from Captain Ted.

"Nothing like it," Captain Dick laughed modestly. "Some one had to win, you know, and the luck came to us."

"Luck!" exploded Ted unbelievingly. "Nothing like it, either. No sheer luck could ever have broken down the cast-iron determination that our fellows had to win. You Centrals are the real ball players of the town——that's the only answer."

Whooping wildly in their glee, scores of Central Grammar boys rushed at Dick Prescott, trying to get at his hand and wring it.

"Please don't fellows," begged Dick, going almost white under the torment, after three or four boys had succeeded in pumping that arm. "You've no idea how sore my arm is."

"It must be," shouted Greg. "Dick told me to kill his arm, if I had to, but to signal for the balls that would strike out three batsmen in lightning order."

"The left hand, then!" clamored more of Dick's admirers. Laughingly, Prescott submitted to having his left hand "shaken" almost out of joint.

"Don't make such a fuss about it, fellows," begged Dick at last. "Remember that we have a permit for a bonfire on this lot to-night, and that the stuff is piled up in the rear of the next yard. You fellows who didn't have to go lame bestir yourselves now in bringing on the old boxes and barrels."

"Whoops!" yelled a Central Grammar boy, starting off. "Bring out the stuff and pile it high."

"Let the Souths help!" bawled Ted Teall at the top of his voice. "No matter who won, we'll all celebrate."

"Ted, you won't play any funny tricks on that pile of wood?" questioned Dick a bit uneasily, as he followed Captain Teall.

"What do you take me for?" demanded the South Grammar boy. "Do you think that I'm not on the level?"

"I'm answered," was Dick Prescott's satisfied answer.

Ere long the material for a monster bonfire was piled. Word was given out that it would be set going just a few minutes after dark.

"We came up here to see what we could find to do, didn't we?" whispered Bert Dodge, nudging Fred Ripley.

"Yes," nodded Fred uneasily; "and, so far, we haven't struck a thing that would be safe to do."

"The dickens we haven't," chuckled Dodge.

"What, then?" Fred inquired. Bert whispered in his ear, adding: "It won't cost us more than a dollar apiece, Fred."

"It's great," declared Ripley enthusiastically. "But we've got to move quickly, and at the right minute, or we'll be caught. I wouldn't give much for our chances of comfort if we're caught in this thing."

"We won't be, or we ought not to be," Dodge retorted. "But we'd better get home and get our suppers on the jump."

"We can do better than that; we can get a quick meal at one of the restaurants and then jump back on the job."

"Rip, you have a great head sometimes," admitted Bert Dodge.

At a time when every one else was at supper Fred Ripley and Bert Dodge stole back to the scene of the bonfire. After glancing cautiously about, they felt sure that no one was observing them. Then they stole close to the pile of combustibles. For a few moments they worked there, removing lids from tin cans and planting them safely out of sight.

Human nature—-of the American brand, at any rate—-dearly loves a bonfire. By dark that evening some two hundred grown-up and several hundred Gridley boys had congregated on the late ball field.

"Touch it off, some one. There's no use in waiting any longer," urged some of the bystanders. "It's almost dark."

"No, no! Wait!" urged Tom Reade. "The blaze will be all the finer after dark."

"Where's Dick Prescott?" sounded a voice, this being followed by a dinning clamor for the captain of the Centrals.

"Here!" called Dick, when he could make himself heard.

"Pouch it off, Dick! Let the fun start. You're the right one to set the bonfire going."

"Not I," Prescott answered. "There is some one else here who has been appointed to set the blaze going, and who has accepted the job."

"Then trot him out and let him get busy!" came the urgent demand.

"Wait just a few minutes, fellows. We want it really dark," urged Captain Prescott.

At last, when he judged it dark enough, Dick stepped forward, Captain Ted Teall at his side.

"Friends," Dick explained, "Teall has been good enough to agree to start the blaze tonight."

"South Grammar fellows this way, please!" called Teall. "Now, friends, please don't any of you make any noise until we Souths have a chance to say just a few words. All ready, South Grammars? Then three cheers for the Central Grammar School, winners of the school baseball league series. Let 'em rip out loudly!"

The cheers were given, followed by a tiger.

"Is Hi Martin, captain of the North Grammar nine, here?" called Ted Teall.

But Hi wasn't, or else he kept his presence very quiet.

"Hi wouldn't he here," jeered some one. "He didn't win—-couldn't win—-and he's sore."

Again Ted called for Hi Martin, though still without success.

"Then I'll have to light the fire alone," Ted declared. "I had hoped that the captains of both of the walloped teams might share the honor."

Tom Reade and Dave Darrin hastily emptied a five-gallon can of oil on the old boxes and barrels and other pieces of wood.

"All clear?" called Ted.

"All clear," nodded Tom Reade.

"Then I'll light the blaze," shouted Ted. "This is a lot easier than winning ball games," he added good-naturedly.

Three or four wind-proof matches Teall struck on a box and tossed into the oil-soaked pile of combustibles. In a moment the increasing heat of the blaze drove him back several yards.

Higher and higher mounted the red and yellow flames. Hundreds stood about, their faces fully illumined by the big glow.

"It's going to be a great one," Ted called to Dick, as the latter came toward him.

"Finest bonfire I've ever seen," Prescott answered.

"But——" began Teall, a puzzled look on his face. Then——sniff! sniff! "Queer stuff, that! What a stuffing smoke it makes. I wonder what it is that burns with such a sharp smell?"

"It must be pitch," replied Dick Prescott, also sniffing. "Whew! How sharp it is!"

Ted began to sneeze. Dick followed suit. Presently all of the boys who were standing at all near the blazing pile found themselves sneezing, coughing or sputtering at a great rate. Some of the men, further away, caught the acrid fumes.

"This is a mean trick some one has played on us," cried Dick, falling back before the stifling odors.

"I hope you don't think I did a mean thing like that?" demanded Teall anxiously.

"I'm sure you didn't," Prescott answered. "You're full of tricks, Ted Teall, but you're a real sportsman after you've been beaten."

"Say, can this possibly be any of Hi Martin's work?" demanded Tom Reade, as the boys fell back steadily from the bonfire.

"Only one objection to suspecting Hi," retorted Teall.

"What's that?" asked Greg. "Too proud?"

"No," snapped Teall. "Hi hasn't brains enough to think up anything."

"This is just like boys. It's really what one gets for turning out to a boys' bonfire!" growled one man between fits of coughing, as he rapidly got away from the fire. It's an abominably mean trick!"

"Who did it?" asked another man.

"Oh, you can't find that out now," replied still another. "You all know the way that boys hang together in mischief. No one would tell you, or dare to tell you, if he knew."

"I'd like to know the boy, for about one minute!" snapped one stout, red-faced man, down whose cheeks the tears were trickling. "It's that loutish trick of putting red pepper on a fire. No one but a feeble-minded boy would think of playing an old, moth-eaten trick like that!"

"It would pay us to get out of here quickly, if any one suspected us," whispered Fred Ripley to his friend.

"Sh! Shut up!" returned Dodge in a hoarse whisper. "It isn't best for us to be seen whispering. Look innocent."

From behind a heavy hand descended abruptly on either coat collar, taking firm hold.

"Here are the young apes who played the trick!" roared an angry voice. "I just heard them whispering about it, and when I was finishing supper I remember that I looked out of the window and saw these boys fooling about the pile."

"What did you put on the fire?" demanded a man, stepping in front of the now frightened youths, who were hemmed in so that they could not escape.

"Red pepper," returned Ripley sullenly. He spoke before he thought, thus admitting his guilt and Dodge's.

"You idiot!" hissed Bert.

"You're both of you idiots," retorted the captor, who had now released both young men. "Besides being a mean, detestable trick, it's as old as the world. That red-pepper trick was invented by some stupid lout who lived thousands of years before the Flood."

"What shall we do with these imps?" demanded a voice.

"There must be some High School boys here," said the man who had first seized the humiliated pair by their collars. "Let the High School boys decide what is to be done with them."

"We don't care what's done with a pair of simpletons like them," spoke up Ben Tozier. "Let the crowd go as far as it likes with such a pair."

"Don't you dare do anything to us" screamed Ripley, now beside himself with rage. "It will go hard with any one who interferes with us.

"Ha! ha! Ho! ho!" roared some of the crowd. "Listen to the half-witted pair!"

While another man spoke up jovially:

"I'll tell you what to do with them. They came here to spoil the fun of the Grammar School boys. Let the Grammar School boys dispose of these stupid fellows as they choose."

"I tell you," raged Ripley, "that it will go hard with any one who interferes with our comfort. There are laws in this land."

"Look at what doesn't want its comfort interfered with!" jeered another voice. "This comes from a lout who interfered with our comfort by putting several cans of red pepper on the bonfire. Turn 'em over to the Grammar School boys. Boys, what do you want to do with this pair?"

"We'll make 'em run the gauntlet," spoke up Spoff Henderson eagerly.

In a twinkling, so it seemed, a long double row of Grammar School boys was formed down the street. Some of these boys had light twigs or sticks; others stood ready to use their hands.

"Start 'em!" yelled Spoff. Some one did start the pair. Bert and Fred sullenly refused to run, but quickly changed their minds. Down the street they raced, Ripley in advance, between two parallel lines of Grammar School boys. Sticks were laid over them, or hands reached out and administered cuffings. It was a grotesque sight. Long before they reached the end of the double line Bert and Fred yelled for mercy, but got none. With final blows they were turned loose and vanished into the night. Within a few minutes the pepper in the bonfire had burned out. Then the revelers drew nearer, piling on other combustible stuff.

Thus was fittingly observed the victory of Dick Prescott's nine in winning the local Grammar School championship.

Chapter XVIII

The reader may be sure that the members of his baseball squad had reminded him of his promise to tell them what the man on the clubhouse steps said.

"I promised I'd tell you, if you won that game," Dick admitted.

"Yes, yes!" the other boys pressed.

"But I didn't say *when* I'd tell you, did I?"

"You're not going to try to sneak out of it that way, are you, Dick?" Dave Darrin demanded, as the boys met on Main Street the following morning, Saturday.

"I'm not going to sneak out of it at all, as you fellows ought to know," Dick replied. "I'm going to tell you——when the proper time comes."

"When will that be?" asked Greg. "And that's all we'll get out of him, no matter how how much we talk!" muttered Tom Reade.

"Here comes Hi Martin," announced Greg. "He has Bill Rodgers with him."

"It can't be about baseball, anyway," said Dick. "I think Hi has his fill of that game."

"Good morning," was Martin's greeting, as he and Rodgers approached. "I have a message for you from North Grammar."

"Deliver it, and we'll sign on the book for it," retorted Reade.

"We're not satisfied to rest the claims of the North Grammar on baseball alone," Hi went on.

"I shouldn't imagine you would be," Dick smiled.

"Therefore we are going to challenge you to another form of contest."

"A talking match?" Tom wanted to know.

"No, sir. I bear from the North Grammar boys a challenge to Central Grammar to meet us in swimming matches in the river. The contests must be so arranged as to show which school may hold the championship in swimming. Are you afraid to meet us in the water?" Hi asked.

"Afraid? No," Dick retorted. "But why didn't you fellows spring this on us earlier? Next week Thursday will be graduating day."

"Well, we can swim the Saturday after," Hi proposed.

"But we'll be graduated then. We won't be Grammar School boys any more," protested Dick.

"Is that the way you're going to get out of the challenge that we've issued?" Martin demanded scornfully.

"No; and you certainly know better," Dick retorted. "But how can we hold a school contest when we're no longer enrolled in the school that we're supposed to represent?" Dick insisted.

"You can if you want to," Hi sneered. "But I can see that you fellows don't care about meeting us in a swimming contest. All right; then I'll go back and tell the North Grammar fellows that Central funks.

"There's a way that we can arrange it, I think," put in Dave Darrin, who had been listening intently. "Dick, why can't we get Old Dut to authorize us to represent Central Grammar within a day or two after graduation? If he says it's all right, then surely, even though we have just graduated, we'll be able to represent our old school."

"We can talk that over with Mr. Jones," Dick nodded.

"My idea is that you fellows are afraid to say 'yes' to our challenge, sneered Martin.

"You may go on thinking that, if it gives you any pleasure," said Dick coolly. "But if you really want our answer, we'll give it to you on Monday afternoon."

"The Monday after Christmas?" jeered Hi.

"We'll give you our answer next Monday afternoon," Dick rejoined a bit stiffly.

"Is the South Grammar to be in this?" asked Dave.

"No; we don't want that crowd," Hi answered quickly before Rodgers could speak.

"Then the contest won't be for the championship of Gridley, will it?" Dick inquired.

"Yes, it will," Hi assured him.

"I don't see how it can be, when it's only between two out of the three Grammar Schools in the town," Dick argued.

"The challenge is issued only to Central Grammar," wound up Hi, turning to leave. "And if you haven't accepted before Monday evening, we of the North

Grammar will hold that you have backed out and don't dare meet us. Oh, by the way, Prescott, you'd better look out for Ripley and Dodge. They mean to get square with you for what happened last night."

"Get square with me for it?" laughed Prescott, unafraid. "All right, but that's rather rich! Why, I had nothing to do with it."

"They blame you a good deal for it," added Hi, "and they declare that they're going to get even with you."

"All right; let them try it," Dick nodded.

"What do you think of this swimming challenge?" asked Dave quickly.

"Why, I think," Dick replied, "that it will bear looking into closely. There may be some trick about it, and we must look out that we are not roped into some funny game. We'll see the fellows at school on Monday."

"Hi Martin is probably the best swimmer among the Grammar School boys of Gridley," Tom suggested.

"I think that he most likely is," Dick agreed. "If he proposes to stand for North Grammar, and wants us to put up one candidate against him, then Hi would probably take the race. If we take the challenge, either we ought to insist on a team race, or else on a number of separate events by different fellows, each event to count for so many points on the score. In any match of singles Hi Martin might win. If we go into this at all, we must look out that it isn't fixed so that Hi Martin, alone, can carry off the championship for his school."

"The very fact that Hi proposed it makes me suspicious that he has some trick in reserve," Tom urged.

"I like the general idea," spoke up Greg. "Any swimming contest that is a real match between the schools, instead of between individuals, will be good sport and arouse a lot of school interest. There are a lot of fairly good swimmers in our school, too."

"We'll talk it over with the fellows, and with Old Dut also," Dick went on. "Of course we have no right to act for the school unless the other fellows are willing."

When Dick left his chums at noon it was with an agreement to meet on Main Street again at half past one.

At fifteen minutes past one the telephone bell rang in the little bookstore.

"Have you a copy of Moore's Ballads?" asked a masculine voice.

"Yes," replied Mr. Prescott; "in different styles of bindings and at different prices."

The bookseller then went on to describe the bindings and named the prices. The customer at the other end of the wire seemed to prefer an expensive volume, which came at four dollars.

"Can you deliver the book immediately, with a bill, to Mrs. Carhart, at the Gideon Wells place?" continued the voice at the other end.

"Yes; I think so," replied Mr. Prescott.

"The book must be delivered within the hour," continued the voice, "as Mrs. Carhart is going on a journey and wishes the book to read while on the train."

"I will deliver the book within fifteen minutes," Mr. Prescott promised. "At the Gideon Wells place, did you say? I didn't know that it had a tenant."

"Mrs. Carhart has taken the place for the summer. I will rely upon you to deliver the book immediately. Thank you; good-bye."

"I suppose you have an appointment with the crowd, Dick," smiled his father, as he hung up the receiver. "I don't like to get in the way of your fun, but I shall have to ask you to deliver the book, for the profit on that volume is too large to be overlooked."

"I don't mind going," Dick answered. "I can get back just a little late. I'm all ready as soon as you have the book wrapped and the bill made out."

Three or four minutes later Dick left the store. At the corner of Main Street he looked to see whether any of his chums were visible, but none were. So he turned and started, traveling fast.

Had young Prescott answered the 'phone call himself he very likely would have suspected that the voice of the customer was that of Bert Dodge disguised. However, as it was, the Grammar School boy had no suspicion whatever. He made part of the distance at a jog trot. He was soon in the less thickly inhabited part of the town, down in a section of large estates, many of which were used only as summer homes.

"This Mrs. Carhart must be a new-comer in Gridley," reflected Dick, as he hastened along. "I hope she'll buy a lot of books of us at as good prices."

He came now to the corner of the Wells estate, the grounds of which were some eighty acres in extent. He passed the corner and ran along toward two great elms that grew just inside the trim wall.

Just as he reached these elms two figures started up from behind the wall beyond. The same two figures leaped over the wall, confronting the Grammar School boy.

"Howdy, Prescott," called Bert Dodge, with a mocking grin.

"We were just saying that we'd rather see you than any one else on earth," leered Fred Ripley, as he stepped in the Grammar School boy's path.

"I haven't any time to waste on you two just now," Prescott answered coldly, trying to step around the pair.

"Then you'll take the time," scoffed Bert, reaching out to seize Dick by the shoulder.

Fred Ripley aimed an unexpected blow that sent the lad to earth and the book flying several feet beyond.

Chapter XIX

"That was just like you—-it was so cowardly and low down!" cried Dick hotly, as he leaped to his feet.

He was now near the package containing the book. Doubtless he could have snatched up the book and sprinted to safety. But that was not his way of meeting so great an affront.

"Don't you get saucy!" warned Fred, edging in closer. Bert Dodge veered around so that be could attack Dick from one side.

"It would be honoring you too much to talk to you in any vein," Dick retorted sarcastically. "You're a pair of the most worthless rowdies in Gridley."

"Go for him, Bert!" called Ripley.

"Why don't you?" sneered Dick, making a leap forward, straight at Ripley.

Dodge swung in from behind, hitting Dick over the head. But Prescott's movement, in the same moment, made the blow only a glancing one.

Bump! Dick landed on Fred Ripley's nose with force and weight enough to make the lawyer's son stagger.

"Pound his head off, Bert!" howled Ripley putting a hand to his injured nose.

But Dick wheeled just in time to avoid a treacherous blow from the rear. With all the fury of the oppressed, Prescott leaped in, planting one foot heavily on some of Bert's toes and striking a blow that landed over that indignant youth's belt-line. Bert fell back, panting.

"If you two have enough now," remarked Dick more coolly, "I'll pick up my package and go on about my business."

"You can wager you won't get away until we've settled with you!" snarled Dodge. "Rip, never mind your nose. Help me close in on this scamp and show him what we can do to a fellow that we don't like."

In another moment Dick was the center of a cyclone, or so it felt to him. Both boys were larger and stronger, even if not quite as quick as he. They rained blows upon him.

"Don't try to holler," jeered Fred Ripley. "That won't do you any good. We'll tell you when you've had enough. Take it from us and never mind your own opinions."

Dick did not answer. Sore and winded, he fought with all the spirit that was in him.

So busy were all three of the boys, that none of them noted the approach of a light express wagon drawn by a single horse. The driver hauled up, a few yards away, then advanced, driving whip in hand.

Slash!

"O-o-o-h!" yelled Fred Ripley, as he felt the whip land on his legs.

Slash! slash!

"Quit that, you fiend!" begged Bert Dodge, doubling up and screaming with pain.

"I'll quit when I think you've had enough!" hissed Dave Darrin, his face ablaze with anger, his eyes flashing fire.

Slash! slash! slash!

Dave plied the whip relentlessly until he had inflicted half a dozen more blows on the legs of each High School boy.

"If you try to run away," warned Dave, "either of you, I'll run after you and lay on ten times as much as I'm giving you."

"Quit, now, Dave," urged Dick, running to his chum and laying a hand on Darrin's active right arm. "They've had lots—-plenty. Such things as they, can't stand a man's dose."

"I'm not a bit tired," retorted Dave ironically. "Besides, I rather enjoy this exercise."

"We'll have you arrested, Dave Darrin!" moaned Ripley.

"You will, eh?" Dave demanded, breaking away from Prescott's restraining hold and making for Fred.

"No, no, no!" cried Ripley, cowering.

"Yes, we will—-you can wager we will!" yelled Dodge from a safer distance.

"Arrested—-for what?" demanded Darrin.

"For assaulting us," returned Bert Dodge. "Oh, you'll catch it!"

"Have I been guilty of any more of an assault than I found you fellows engaged in", Dave asked coolly. "Don't you think you'd look rather funny in court when it was known why I laid the whip over you?"

"We'll get the better of you, just the same," yelled Ripley, who had now retreated to the side of his friend and felt bolder. "My father's a lawyer——the smartest in the town."

"And he's also a gentleman," broke in Dick. "I wish his son took after him. As for arrest——and trouble in court——bosh! Try it on!"

Prescott now walked coolly to where his little package lay, and found it uninjured.

"How did you happen to come along on the wagon?" Dick asked, as Fred and Bert limped away from their Waterloo.

"One of the express company's drivers was late coming back from dinner, and there was a package that had to be delivered at once," Darrin answered. "The manager offered me ten cents to make the delivery. I am glad that I took the job. Where are you going?"

"In there," Prescott answered, pointing to the house. "I've got to deliver this book collect to a Mrs. Carhart."

"Get up on the seat and I'll drive you in there," proposed Dave. "Though I don't believe there's any one living in the house. All the front doors and windows are boarded up."

After five minutes of doorbell ringing Dick concluded that he would find no Mrs. Carhart there.

"I guess I understand," nodded Prescott. "Either Dodge or Ripley must have sent that 'phone message. That was their way to get me alone where they could both handle me without much danger of interference."

"It turned out finely——for them," chuckled Dave, as both boys climbed back to the seat of the wagon. "But say, do you think they could really make any trouble for me for using the whip over them?"

"I don't know. I don't believe they'll try, anyway," Dick answered thoughtfully. "It wouldn't be very nice for Fred to have his father find out how his son spends his time and pocket money."

Dave drove back to Main Street, letting Dick off at his corner. Down the side street a few doors and into the bookshop he hurried.

"Back again?" was Mr. Prescott's greeting. "What was the matter——the volume not satisfactory!"

"No such party at the address," his son answered. "But I think I can explain why the order was 'phoned in."

Dick then proceeded to narrate what had happened. His father listened with

114

growing anger.

"What a low, worthless trick that was to play," he cried. "Dick, if you'll stay here and attend the store I'll step around to Mr. Ripley's office and speak to him about it. Then I'll go over to the bank and see Bert's father."

"Don't, dad; please don't," begged the boy.

"It seems to me that such action is highly necessary," maintained Mr. Prescott.

"I hope you won't do it, dad. The best way to treat boys' rows is to let them settle among themselves. If you interfere in this matter, dad, I shall get a name among other boys for running to my father for protection. That will turn the laugh on me all over town. I'd much rather fight my own battles and take an occasional pounding."

"Well, perhaps you're right about it," admitted his father thoughtfully. "At all events, I'm glad to see that your disposition is to take care of your own troubles. I won't interfere, though I am certain that Mr. Ripley would like to know something about this affair."

"I already do know something about it," gravely announced a voice behind them. There stood Lawyer Ripley, who had dropped in to buy a magazine.

"I shall be glad if you will tell me more about this," the lawyer went on solemnly.

Gladly would Dick have gotten out of it. He was inclined to say very little, though what he did say was added to by his father.

"Is this the book, in this package?" inquired Mr. Ripley, as be picked up the parcel.

"Yes," nodded Mr. Prescott.

"And the price?"

"Four dollars."

"Mr. Prescott, kindly charge this book to my account, unless I return it by Monday morning," the lawyer went on. "I shall try to see young Darrin this afternoon. Then I shall question my son when I return home. I don't consider it fair to condemn him unheard, but if I find that he had such a part in this afternoon's affair as has been described, then I shall tell him that he is bound to take goods that he has any part in ordering. In that connection, when I hand him his next allowance of pocket money, I shall keep out four dollars and hand him the book in place thereof. That ought to make him rather careful about ordering goods in which he is not really interested."

"But, as I now recall the voice over the telephone," urged Mr. Prescott, "I am inclined to think that it was young Dodge's voice, disguised, that I heard."

"If my son had any share in the transaction, it will make no difference," replied Lawyer Ripley very gravely. "This book will then become a part of his small library, and at his own personal expense. I thank you both. Good afternoon."

"Well, of all the queer turn-overs, that's the best!" grinned Dick appreciatively, after the lawyer had gone. "Wouldn't I like to see Rip when he gets that book of ballads handed him as the larger part of his pocket allowance!"

"It's certainly a clever way for his father to handle the affair," smiled Mr. Prescott. "However, in making the charge for the book I shall deduct the profit. Like yourself, son, I don't want to profit by tale-bearing. And now, why not run out and see if you can find your young friends? I don't believe I shall need you further this afternoon."

Inwardly Dave Darrin was a good bit disturbed when, a few minutes later, Lawyer Ripley walked into the express office and inquired for him. Fred's father asked a good many questions, which Dave answered truthfully though reluctantly.

"Assuming that the affair was as you describe, Darrin," stated the legal man at last, "I wish to thank you for teaching the young man what must have been a needed lesson."

When Dave learned from Dick, a little later, the story of Fred's unintentional purchase of a four-dollar book, there was a big laugh.

Chapter XX

"See no reason why you can't represent this school in an athletic meet a day or two after graduation," said Old Dut, when asked about it. "If the North Grammar boys believe they excel at that sport, they should be given a chance. Naturally they are disappointed over finding themselves at the bottom of the list in baseball."

"Go after 'em to-day, Dick!" yelled the boys. "Perhaps we can beat them in the water, too."

"Find Hi Martin this afternoon and settle it," added others.

"I won't serve alone," Dick retorted, shaking his head. "If you fellows want me to serve on a committee and will give us full powers to act, I'm willing."

"I think that will be the best way to go about it, boys," approved Old Dut. "There should be a committee, and then you must be prepared to stand by any arrangements that the committee may make."

"What's the matter with choosing a committee of ten?" proposed Toby Ross.

"Too many," smiled Old Dut wisely.

"There'd be too much talking then. A committee should have but a very few members."

"Are nominations in order?" queried Spoff Henderson.

"Yes," nodded Old Dut. "Since I've been consulted, I'll preside at this yard meeting."

"Then I nominate Dick Prescott, Dave Darrin and Greg Holmes," Spoff continued.

"Second the motion," called Ross.

Old Dut put the motion, which was carried. "As Master Prescott was first named," announced the principal, "he will naturally be the chairman of the committee."

"I move the committee have full powers in arranging for the race," Spoff added.

This was also carried. That afternoon, when school was out, the boys hurried along Main Street, keeping a sharp lookout for Hi. At last they espied him, with Bill Rodgers.

"What are you going to do about the swimming race?" called Hi from across the street.

"This is our committee, duly appointed by the Central Grammar boys," Dick called back. "When will your committee be ready?"

"We're ready now," answered Hi. "Come over here and we'll talk about it."

Hi leaned against the fence on his own side of the street, determined not to concede anything to the Central Grammar boys.

"Have you two been regularly appointed as a committee?" asked Prescott.

"We don't have to be," Hi answered indifferently. "We know whatwe're talking about."

"You'll have to be regularly appointed by your school before we'll talk with you," Dick retorted.

"You're afraid to meet us in a swimming match," Hi jeered.

"So afraid," Prescott answered, "that we've appointed a committee regularly; but you fellows, who have been doing all the talking, aren't willing to get together and elect a regular committee to represent your school."

"You're afraid, I tell you," sneered Hi, while Bill Rodgers grinned.

"No; we're ready to arrange the match when your school sends a regular committee."

"Come on over here and talk it over, if you're not afraid," urged Hi Martin.

"We can't talk it over with you, as you've admitted that you don't represent your school."

"Well, then, we do represent it," claimed Hi.

"That statement comes too late. Hi, we'll meet you at this same place at half past four to-morrow afternoon. If you fail to show up it will be all off. And your committee will have to bring a note, signed by your principal, naming the members of your committee and stating that it has been regularly appointed. We'll bring the same from our principal.

"I guess the swimming match between the two schools is all off, then," yawned Martin. "You fellows don't want to go into it, for you know you'd be beaten stiff. That's why you try to hedge behind a committee."

"It's all off if you fellows don't go at it in a regular way," Dick contended firmly. "We're not going to enter a match and then find that you and Bill Rodgers represent no one but yourselves."

"What's all the noise about?" good-naturedly asked Reporter Len Spencer, who, turning the corner, had halted behind Prescott and his friends.

Dick explained the situation.

"Prescott is right," decided Len. "Martin, if the boys at your school are not enough in earnest to arrange the contest through an authorized committee, then folks will understand that the North Grammar didn't really want a swimming contest."

"But we do want one," blustered Martin.

"Then go about it in a regular way, after consulting your principal, as the Central Grammar boys have done," urged Len. "And, instead of meeting here on a corner, you can meet at my desk at the 'Blade' office."

Hi Martin was "stumped" at this point, and he knew it. If he backed out now he would make himself and his school ridiculous.

"All right," agreed the North Grammar boy reluctantly.

"Don't forget to bring a note from your principal to the effect that the boys named are the regular school committee," Dick called after him.

"We'll do the thing in our own way," Hi retorted. "Come along, Bill."

"I thought Martin might be up to some tricks," muttered Dick Prescott.

"If he is, tricks won't help him or his school," laughed Len. "We'll see this thing put through in regular shape."

So, on Tuesday afternoon, Dick and his fellow members of the committee were at the "Blade" office punctually.

At ten minutes past the time no boy from the North Grammar had appeared.

"You won't have to wait much longer," smiled Len. "It looks as though the North Grammar boys were bluffing."

At ten minutes of five Dick and his chums rose to leave the "Blade" office.

"Wait a minute," urged Len at the door. "I believe I see your rivals coming now."

Hi Martin, Bill Rodgers and Courtney Page strolled rather indolently up to the door and entered.

"You're late," said Len crisply. "If you boys go into a race, I believe you'll be just as late at the finish."

"There wasn't any use in hurrying," grunted Eel. "There's lots of the day left."

"Unless you regard an appointment as a gentlemen's agreement, and to be kept," marked Len Spencer, rather severely. "I have been giving up my time to this affair of yours, and my time is worth something. But take seats. Have you boys any paper to show that you represent your school?"

"Yes," admitted Hi, producing an envelope. "Our principal gives us the proper authority."

Len read the note, nodding. "The Central Grammar boys have also produced their authority to act, so now we can get down to the details of the contest. The North Grammar boys are the challengers, are they not?"

"Yes," claimed Hi.

"Then what sort of a swimming contest do you propose?" Len asked.

"Each school to appoint its best swimmer, and arrange a half-mile race between the champions of the two schools," Hi answered promptly. "The school whose champion wins is to be declared the champion in swimming."

"We expected that," nodded Dick, "and we won't agree to it. If this match is to be held for the school championship, then there should be several boys entered from each school——say five, six or seven from each school. Then the contest would really represent the schools."

"But one boy would win, just the same, in any case," retorted Martin. "What difference would it make?"

"The way that I propose," urged Dick, "no single boy could win for his school. Suppose we enter seven boys from each school. Then the school whose seven boys are in ahead of the seven boys on the other side will win the contest. In other words, of the fourteen swimmers, one is bound to come in last of all. The school to which this last-in swimmer belongs is the school that loses the match."

"Huh! I don't see anything in that idea," retorted Hi. "That, perhaps, wouldn't mean anything at all for the school that happened to have the one best swimmer of all."

"It would make it impossible for either school to enter one real swimmer and six dummies, and still win the match," Dick argued. "My plan will stop the contest from being a one-boy race and will give the contest to the school that has the best average swimmers."

"Huh! I don't see it," said Hi doggedly.

"I think Prescott has the better of the argument," broke in Len Spencer, who had sat tapping his desk with a pencil.

"Then I don't care much for your idea, either, Spencer," retorted Martin.

"It may be that my idea isn't any good," nodded Len indulgently. "I won't even claim that I know anything about sports. But you must surely know who the umpire is in any such dispute. It's always the editor of the local paper. So, Martin, if you won't agree with Prescott, and if you won't admit that I know anything about it either, suppose we lay the question before the editor of the 'Blade.' I think he's in just now."

"As for me," spoke up Bill Rodgers, breaking his silence, "it seems to me that Prescott's idea is good and fair."

"What do you say to that kind of stuff, Page?" inquired Hi quickly.

"I——I——er——well, I am agreeable to anything that pleases the rest of you," stammered Courtney Page, by nature, a sail trimmer.

"You're a chump, then," Hi retorted elegantly. "The whole reason why Prescott objects to one boy representing each school is that he's afraid I can out-swim any boy that Central Grammar can produce."

"And I take it, Martin," Dick retorted, "that your reason for insisting on the one-boy race, is due to your belief that you can win from any one boy. Very likely you are the fastest and strongest swimmer in any Gridley school. But a race with seven boys on a side will better represent the average abilities of the two schools. In baseball we tried to find out which school had the average best players. We didn't try simply to find out which school could boast of the one star player."

"That's right," nodded Len Spencer.

"Prescott, you're afraid to race with me, you or any other one fellow in Central Grammar!" exclaimed Hi indignantly.

"No; I'm not afraid to swim against you," Dick declared quietly. "I won't have the championship between the two schools rest on any such race, but I'll enter a separate race against you——any distance——this in addition to a seven-fellow race between the schools."

"Now, I guess you haven't a leg left to stand on, Martin," smiled Spencer. "Prescott proposes a seven-fellow race between the schools, the school responsible for the last man who comes in to lose the contest. That is to be for the school championship. Then, if you think you can outswim Prescott, he agrees to enter an individual and personal race with you."

"If Prescott and I swim against each other, then we won't swim in the seven-fellow race, anyway." protested Hi.

"I'll agree to that," Dick nodded.

After some more talking the details were arranged. Len reduced them to writing and the committees for both schools signed.

"I'll publish this in the 'Blade' to-morrow morning," said Spencer. "Then the whole town will know the terms of the race."

Friday, if pleasant, was the date chosen, the seven-fellow race to begin as soon as possible after two P.M., the personal race between Prescott and Martin to follow. Such details as choosing the officials of the race were to be left to the principals of the two schools.

"It's all settled, then, gentlemen," said Spencer, rising and holding out his right hand. "If you don't see me before you may be sure of my being on hand to report the races themselves. I shall do all I can to encourage schoolboy sports in Gridley. I've a notion, too, that there will be on hand Friday a goodly showing of High School athletes. The young men of the High School will naturally want to look over the contestants and see who is going to make good material for the High School teams."

"I'm thankful to say," retorted Hi stiffly, "that I do not expect to attend Gridley High School. My father is going to send me to one of the best prep. schools in the country. Page and Rodgers are going to good schools, too."

"I hope none of your fathers will be disappointed," remarked Spencer gravely. "Personally, I consider the Gridley High School one of the best schools in the United States."

"It will do, of course, for those who really can't afford to go to better and more select schools," Hi conceded. "Prescott, look out that you don't get drowned when you're practicing to beat me on Friday."

"I'm not really sure that I shall practice swimming before Friday," Dick smiled in answer. "I'm going to be pretty busy until after graduation."

"Dick," asked Greg seriously, when the three chums were by themselves, "have you any idea in the world that you can win out against Hi Martin?"

"Oh, I may not win," Prescott replied. "Yet, if I don't I'll promise you to be the hardest pace-maker that Hi Martin ever had behind him in the water."

Chapter XXI

Boys attired in their best tip-toed about in creaking new shoes, resplendently polished for the occasion. Every boy had a flower in his upper button-hole.

Exhibition Hall, usually so bare and barnlike in appearance, was now a jungle of potted plants and ferns, with clumps of bright flowers everywhere.

Over the broad stage hung a fourteen-foot American flag. Flags of other nations, in smaller bits of bunting, trailed off on either side. The piano stood before the center of the stage, down on the floor. Grouped near were the music stands and chairs for other members of the orchestra on this festal day of graduation.

Here and there women teachers still superintended little squads of girls who were putting on the last bright touches of ornamentation. One teacher was drilling a dozen much-dressed-up boys of the seventh grade, who were to act as ushers on this great Thursday afternoon. It was half an hour before the doors were to be opened.

Curiously enough, there were no eighth-grade pupils present. These were assembled in Room 1, on the floor below, seated behind the desks that had been theirs during the school year.

"Young ladies and gentlemen," began Old Dut, rapping on his desk and rising. As he looked about there was a curious expression on his face, and some water in his twinkling eyes.

"I am going to take occasion to say the last few words that I shall have a chance to say to you confidentially and in private," continued the principal. "I am conscious that I am taking one of my last looks at you all as my pupils. I might call this the dying class, if it were not for the fact that, for most of you, to-day will be the real birth. You will go forth into the world to-day, the larger portion of you. You will leave school behind and tackle the world as budding men and women. You will begin soon to grapple with the work, the problems, the toil——the tears and the joys that come with the beginnings of grown-up life. Those of you who are to be favored with a chance to go further in your education, and who will be schoolboys and schoolgirls yet a while, I most sincerely congratulate. For those who, on the other hand, will step straight from Exhibition Hall into the world of work——aye, and the world of deeds and triumphs, too——I bid you to be of good cheer and courage!

"Be bold, true and loyal! If you have any wonder, any misgivings as to what the world and life may have in store for you, I tell you that these are questions that you will decide mainly for yourselves. It's the hardest thing in this universe to down any man or woman who faces grown-up life with a good and honest claim on the good things of existence. Yet on this subject one word more. Uprightness of heart, of word and deed are not alone sufficient. There is one more great quality that you must link with general honesty and loyalty. Castle Great cannot be stormed except by those who move forward with backbone——Courage! Be bold, steadfast, unwavering. Never lose anything that you justly want through fear that you can't get it. Go after it! The soldier is the type of courage and a good one. Yet you don't find more than one of our soldiers of life in a military uniform. There are soldiers, boys, in every crowd that you mingle with on the street. Be one of them yourselves!

"Boys, be brave, but be gentle. Remember that the bravest men are gentle as any woman. As a soldier proves his courage by his conquests, so must you prove your courage, if you have any to show, by your achievements in the life that starts to-morrow for most of you. Honor and courage! Together they will carry you to lofty heights. If you fail, then reflect that you don't possess these two qualities of manhood. Get these qualities——at no matter what cost——and start out again to victory.

"Girls, be women. Stop and think what it means to be women. All the sweetest, truest and gentlest attributes of the human race. Be women, every minute of your lives, and you will have reached heights where not even the most soldierly boys may follow you. Be women, and the men of our race will reverence and honor you.

"Young ladies and gentlemen, this day comes to me once in every year. It is an old practice with me, as I see each class go forth in our last hour together, to feel that I am watching the departure of the best and truest class that I have yet taught. But this year I am moved more than ever to that feeling. There are those among you who have shown me traits of character that have filled me with even more much more than my usual amount of faith in the future of the American nation. Young ladies and gentlemen, my fellow citizens, permit me to thank you for your loyal work to make this graduating class what it is, and what it is destined to become. Go forth to uphold the traditions of Gridley and the glory of America, and may God bless you, one and all."

His voice rather husky, and his eyes a little more wet, Old Dut sank back into the well-worn chair from which he had taught so many eighth-grade classes.

"Three cheers for our principal!" proposed Danny Grin. The cheers were given lustily, with half a dozen tigers.

"Master Dalzell," replied Old Dut, "coming from the boy who, as the records show, has been disciplined more frequently in the last year than any other pupil present, I consider that a tribute indeed."

"I meant it," said Dan simply.

Later the pupils of the five upper grades marched solemnly into Exhibition Hall, the appearance of the graduating class being greeted with applause by enthusiastic relatives and friends. The orchestra played triumphal marches until all had marched in to their seats.

Then the orchestra paused, only to begin a moment later with the first measures of the opening chorus, sung by more than three hundred youthful voices. It was the usual medley, contributed by pupils who could really sing and by others who really couldn't. An undertone of varying discord ran along under the truer melody.

Then, after his name had been called by the principal, Dick Prescott rose. Very stiff and starched, and painfully conscious of the creaking of his shoes as he went forward in that awesome stillness, Dick ascended the platform, advanced to the front center, made an elaborate bow, and then, in an almost scared voice he began to tell the assembled hundreds of grown-ups why they were there as though they didn't know already. This performance, which admitted of very few gestures, was stated on the programme to be "The Salutatory." From his being chosen to render this address, it was easily to be inferred that Dick was regarded as the brightest boy of the class.

Then other exercises followed. Two members of the Board of Education also had pieces to speak. One told of the educational policy and methods followed in the Gridley schools, on which subject he knew vastly less than any of the eight smiling teachers present. The other member of the Board of Education gave a lot of chilled advice to the members of the graduating class, he did this at much greater length and with far less effect than Old Dut had lately done in his last private talk with his class.

There were a lot of other pieces to be spoken, most of them by the youngsters. There were songs, also exercises in vocal gymnastics. Pupils of the lower classes displayed their expertness at mental arithmetic. Then, after more singing, the superintendent of schools, who had just arrived, mounted the platform and presented each graduating one with a diploma, showing that the recipients had faithfully and successfully completed their Grammar School course.

More music, after which Laura Bentley, a pretty little vision in white cloud effects, with yards of pink ribbon for the sunshine, stepped to the platform, made her bow and launched into the valedictory.

"And now," called Old Dut from the audience, "the old eighth grade is no more. The exercises are over. I thank all who have contributed to make this occasion so pleasant."

"Three cheers for Old—-Mr. Jones, the principal!" yelled Dan Dalzell, as the scrambling to get out began. Needless to say, the cheers were given. Now that the ordeal was over, it was nothing to the discredit of fine Old Dut that the youngsters would have cheered a yellow dog had they been so requested.

Old Dut had slipped down to the egress. There he shook hands with each graduate, wishing them all possible success in life.

"And be sure to come back to these exhibitions whenever you can in after years," the principal called as the last members of the late class were going down the stairs.

"Dick," chuckled Harry Hazelton, as they descended, "when Old Dut was calling on you to go forward and do your little stunt, did you notice the fly on the left side of his nose that he was trying to brush off without letting any one see the move? Ha, ha, ho!"

"Shut up, Hazy," growled Prescott almost savagely. "Haven't you any idea of reverence? We're going down these steps for the last time as Central Grammar boys. I'd rather do it in silence, and thoughtfully."

"Isn't Dickins the queer old chap?" demanded Harry Hazelton, falling back by Reade's side.

"It's a pity you couldn't be queer, just for once, and hold your tongue until we are outside the good old schoolyard," grunted Tom.

"They're a pair of cranks," muttered Harry to Dave Darrin.

"Imitate 'em for once," Darry advised dryly. "Remember, it's the cranks who make the world go around."

For the most part, both boys and girls got their hats very quietly. Then they passed out into the open, walked across the yard and gathered in little groups outside, each holding his beribboned diploma in his right hand.

"It's all over," sighed Tom Reade outside the gate. "Somehow, I wish that I had another year to go—-or else that I'd been a little more decent to Old Dut."

"It was a good old school," sighed Dick, looking back almost regretfully. "And, by the way——-"

"Speech, Dick!" cried a dozen of the boys, crowding around him.

"Get out!" laughed Prescott. "I spoke my piece two hours ago."

Yet the boys continued to crowd about him.

"He's going to tell us now what the man on the clubhouse steps said!" proclaimed Danny Grin hopefully.

Chapter XXII

"Do you fellows really want to know what the man on the clubhouse steps said?" Prescott asked, looking about him with a tantalizing smile.

"Do we?" came in a chorus.

"Hurry up and tell us!"

"Quit your kidding," begged Tom Reade. "Dick, we've waited for months to have the mystery solved. Now, surely, we ought to know. Look at these diplomas; they certify that we know everything else. So trot on the speech of the man on the clubhouse steps."

"Or look for trouble!" added Harry Hazelton warningly.

Dick appeared to hesitate. The boys around him, highly curious, thought he was debating within himself whether or not to give the desired information.

"Come, get swift," desired Spoff Henderson.

"See here, fellows, I'll tell you what I'll do," proposed Dick at last.

"You'll tell us what the man on the clubhouse steps said," broke in Toby Ross.

"Yes," Dick agreed; "but you'll have to let me do so on my own conditions and in my own way. You see this diploma?" holding it up. "I've been working hard for eight years to win this document. Now I'm going to hurry home and put this in a place of safety. After that I'll put on my everyday clothes, and then I'll meet you at the usual corner on Main Street at five o'clock. If any of you fellows really want to know, then, what the man on the clubhouse steps said, I'll tell you."

"You won't postpone telling us, and you won't try to crawl out of it?" pressed Dave Darrin.

"On my honor, I won't," Dick promised.

"On your honor, you won't tell us what the man on the clubhouse steps said?" demanded Tom Reade suspiciously.

"On my honor, I won't try to dodge out of it, or postpone it a minute beyond five o'clock. On my honor I'll tell you, at five o'clock, to-day, what the man on the clubhouse steps said."

"Good!" cried many voices.

"Will many of you be there?" Dick inquired.

"We'll all be there," declared Spoff Henderson. "But, remember, Dick Prescott, you're in honor bound to tell us at last."

"You won't find me dodging or up to any tricks," Dick agreed solemnly. "Until five o'clock, then."

Dick started along. At first quite a crowd went with him, but by degrees the number decreased until only his own five immediate chums were with him.

"Say," suggested Reade suddenly, "since you're going to make a public, show of this, Dick, you ought to let our little crowd in on a private view."

"What do you mean?" Prescott quizzed.

"You know well enough what I mean," Tom retorted. "You ought to tell our own little crowd in advance what the man on the clubhouse steps said."

"Do you really think so?" Prescott asked.

"I do," affirmed Tom.

"And so do the rest of us," asserted Dave Darrin.

"Well———" Dick paused hesitatingly.

"Come, hurry up!" begged Greg.

"It's no more than fair to us," insisted Dan.

"On the whole," Dick continued, "I don't believe it would be fair to the other fellows."

"You big tease!" blurted Harry Hazelton indignantly.

"No; I don't mean to tease you," Dick rejoined, his eyes twinkling. "But I believe in playing fair in life. Don't you, fellows?"

"What has this to do with being fair?" demanded Tom.

"Why, just this: I promised to tell you all at five o'clock. Now, if I were to tell a special few before that time, it would be a bit unfair!"

"Not a bit," retorted Dave. "You've had us dangling from the string longer than you have the rest of the crowd. Therefore, we ought to know the answer before the other fellows."

"It's a question of conscience with me," Dick replied soberly.

"Humph!" snorted Tom. "Well, I suppose we may as well give it up, fellows. The only way we could worm it out of Dick would be to rub his nose in the dirt. And he might fight if we did. This is where I have to leave you. So long! I'll meet the army at five o'clock."

Smiling broadly, Dick went on his way home. He put away his diploma, next removing his best suit and laying it carefully away. Then he donned his more accustomed clothes and ran down to the store.

"It was a very enjoyable exhibition, Dick," said his father.

"And I suppose our son feels that he's a man now?" smiled Mrs. Prescott.

"No; I'm not, mother, and I don't want to be in any hurry, either. There's too much fun in being a boy. And now I've an appointment to meet a lot of the fellows."

"Don't let that appointment make you forget supper time," his mother called after him.

Spoff Henderson and Toby Ross were already at the place of appointment.

"Here comes Dick!" called Spoff. "Now, tell us."

"Wait until the crowd gets here." returned Prescott.

"Ain't you the mean one?" growled Toby. "And we ran all the way home and back."

"Too much hurry is said to be one of the greatest American sins," laughed Dick.

"Well, you're going to tell us, anyway, aren't you?" pressed Spoff.

"Yes; but give the crowd a chance to get here."

Dave and Dan came along, then Tom, Harry and Greg. Tolman and a few other fellows hurried up.

"You might tell us all about that business, now," suggested Tolman.

"I see some more fellows coming up the street," Prescott replied.
"I don't have to tell more than once."

Five minutes later there were more than thirty boys at the corner, and still others were in sight, coming from both ways.

"Say, get busy, Prescott!" called some of the newer corners.

"Let the crowd all get here," Dick insisted.

Presently the crowd numbered more than fifty a lot of their elders, seeing such an unusual crowd of youths on one corner, halted curiously near by.

Then Reporter Len Spencer came along.

"What's all the excitement?" demanded Len, ever keen for local news. One of the boys exclaimed to him what was in the wind.

"Then you'd better hurry up with your statement, Dick," Len advised. "There'll be a riot here soon."

"Five o'clock was the time named," Prescott rejoined.

Just then the town clock began to strike.

"It's five o'clock now, Dick," called Greg.

"Yes," nodded Dick, "and I'm ready at last to redeem my promise."

"He's going to tell us!"

"Hurrah!"

"Shut up! We want to hear."

"You are all assembled here," Prescott continued, "to hear just what it was that the man on the clubhouse steps said."

"Cut out the end-man explanations. Give us the kernel!" shouted one boy.

"What the man on the clubhouse steps said," Dick went ahead, "should be a model to everyone. It is of especial value to all who are tempted to talk too fast and then to think an hour later."

"Yes, but what *did* he say——the man on the clubhouse steps?" howled Harry Hazelton.

"You will know, in a minute," Dick assured his hearers. "Yet, before telling you, I want to impress upon you that, whenever you are tempted to be angry, to be harsh in judgments, or when you can think only ill of your neighbor, then you should always hark back to just what the man on the clubhouse steps said."

There was a pause and silence, the latter broken by Danny Grin demanding impatiently:

"Well, what did he say?"

"You see," Dick explained, "the man was all alone on the clubhouse steps."

"Yes, yes."

"And he wasn't exactly sociable by nature."

"Go on!"

"As I have explained," smiled Dick Prescott, "the man on the clubhouse steps was alone, and——"

"Get ahead faster!"

"So, being alone, he just naturally said——"

"Well?" breathed the auditors. "Well?"

"He just naturally said——*nothing!*"

"What?"

Dick dodged back, laughing. There were a few indignant vocal explosions among the assembled youngsters, followed by dangerous calm and quiet.

"Whenever you find yourself under trying circumstances, or when anger is surging within you, fellows, believe me, you'll always find it wiser to say just what the man on the clubhouse steps said——which was nothing," Dick urged.

"And you got us all the way up here, at an appointed time, just to hear that?" demanded Spoff Henderson.

"It's worth the time it has cost you," Dick urged.

"Rush him fellows!" bawled Toby Ross. "Don't let him escape!"

Indeed, there was no time or chance for getting away. Dick Prescott was rushed, caught and pinned.

"What'll we do with him?" rose the chorus.

"To the fountain! Duck him!"

With a cheer the boys started, carrying Dick along on the shoulders of a few tightly-wedged boys.

Dick's chums made no effort to rescue him. Indeed, perhaps they felt that he deserved what was right ahead of him. But they ran along in the press of boisterous lads.

Len Spencer, grinning hard, rushed along at the head of the juvenile mob.

"Boys, you'd better reconsider!" shouted the young reporter. "Don't write yourselves down as louts. The man on the clubhouse steps, on account of just what he said, proved himself one of the sages of the ages. Prescott, in telling you just what he said, has performed a public service, if only you fellows were bright enough to comprehend."

"Get out of our way, Spencer!" ordered Spoff Henderson. "As sure as guns we're going to duck Dick Prescott in the public fountain."

"If you won't listen to reason, then," roared Len, using his long legs to put him well in advance of the juvenile mob, "then I'll use enchantment to spoil your foolish work. You shall not duck Prescott! Hi, pi, yi, animus, hocus pocus! That enchantment will foil you!"

Having reached the fountain, Len drew aside dramatically.

"In with him!" shouted the youngsters.

Then they halted in sheer amazement. For the first time the boys noted that no water was running in the fountain, and that the basin underneath was wholly dry.

"My enchantment has worked," chuckled Len.

"How did you do it?" demanded one puzzled youngster.

"Never mind," Len retorted mysteriously. "Now, if you don't instantly put Dick Prescott on his feet and leave him alone, I'll work an enchantment that will raise hob with every boy who lays as much as a finger on Dick."

So Prescott was allowed to slide down to his feet. He was laughing, enjoying every moment of the fun.

"We could have run him down to the next fountain," suggested one of the schoolboys.

"It would do you no good, and Prescott no harm," Len retorted dryly. "At three o'clock this afternoon the fire department turned off all of the public fountains in order to clean 'em."

Now Dick's late tormentors began to feel that they had been badly "sold" all around. After the manner of boys, they grinned sheepishly, then more broadly and finally ended by laughing heartily. But the crowd did not break up at once. All waited, with a vague hope that some kind of mischief would happen.

A smaller boy went by, calling the evening newspaper. Tom Reade bought one and stood at the edge of the crowd, reading.

"Here comes Hi Martin!" called someone. That youth had just turned a corner, swinging from his left hand a pudgy rubber bag of the kind that is used for holding a wet bathing suit.

"Hello, Prescott," was Hi's greeting. "Are you all ready to be left behind in the spray tomorrow?"

"If you can leave me there," Dick smiled. "Been out for a practice swim, have you?"

"Yes," nodded Hi; "and if you had seen my speed this afternoon you'd have been scared away from the river for to-morrow."

"Well, I hope one of us wins," grinned Dick.

"One of us?" sniffed Hi. "Of course, one of us has to win when there are only us two in that race. And, after I beat you to-morrow," Hi added consequentially, "I'll be off and away for a good time. Saturday father is going to take our family to New York for three weeks."

"Going to stop at one of the big hotels there?" Reade inquired, looking up from his newspaper.

"Of course we are," Hi rejoined, swelling out his chest. "We shall stop at one of the biggest and finest hotels in the city."

"Then don't get a room too high up from the ground," advised Tom. "I've just been reading in the evening paper that the city authorities in New York have taken all the elevators out of all the biggest hotels."

"Why?" demanded Hi.

"The paper says it's because the elevators are considered too dangerous," Tom replied innocently.

"I don't believe it," scoffed Hi. "Why, how could people get up to their rooms on the fifteenth or eighteenth floor of one of the skyscraper hotels?"

"Oh, well," Tom replied artlessly, "according to the paper the hotels are all going to be equipped with safety-raisers."

"Safety-razors?" demanded Hi Martin blankly. "You idiot, what good would safety-razors be for getting people up twenty floors in a hotel?"

There was a moment's pause. Then a few chuckles came, followed by a few more.

"Whoop!" yelled Danny Grin. Snatching the bathing suit bag from Hi's hand, Dalzell got a good hold on the tie strings, then swung the bag, bringing it down on the top of Hi's head.

"Run along home, Martin!" jeered Dan. "If don't tumble before bed time, then ask your father how it is that dangerous elevators can be replaced with safety-raisers. Here's your bag. Scoot—-before an idea hits you!"

Red-faced and angry, but still puzzled, Hi snatched at his bathing suit bag and hastily decamped.

"Now he'll beat you at swimming or die tomorrow," predicted Dave grimly.

Chapter XXIII

Thanks to Len Spencer's interest in schoolboy athletics, there was a goodly crowd gathered at the river bank the next afternoon. Many people came out in boats. There were at least a dozen launches, including the one that bore Len Spencer, who had been chosen to conduct the races.

The owner of a two room boathouse which adjoined a long wharf had yielded to Spencer's request for a loan of this property. In the boathouse the two school teams disrobed and donned their bathing suits.

Dave Darrin had been called upon to captain the swimming squad from the Central Grammar. With him were Tom, Greg, Dan, Harry, Henderson and Ross. It was as good and representative a team as Central Grammar could furnish.

Bill Rodgers captained the squad from North Grammar. Bill had had his fellows three times in the water, and was proud of them.

Just ten minutes before the time for calling the contestants Dave Darrin led his squad from the boathouse. Out along the pier they ran and dived in.

"The water's just fine for swimming to-day," ecstatically remarked Tom Reade, as he came up, blew the water from his mouth and took a few strokes. "In fact, the water's too fine."

"Too fine?" queried Dave. "How so?"

"Why, it makes a fellow feel so fine," retorted Tom, "that I'm afraid it will make us all winners, and then there won't be any glory for either school."

The North Grammar boys now splashed in. Len Spencer, who had just seen to the placing of the further stake boat, now returned in the launch.

Both the squad race and the individual contest were to be for a quarter of a mile straightaway, with the start from a moored raft down the river.

"Every one pile aboard!" called Len, the launch that he was on gliding in at the pier. Wet swimmers dropped into the launch until it was filled. Then another small gasoline craft took aboard the left-overs. The crowd preferred to remain at this end of the course to see the finish.

"It won't take North Grammar long to wind your crowd up in the water," declared Hi Martin, as he and Dick stood at the end of the pier watching the departure. Both were already in their bathing costumes.

"Maybe not," Dick assented. "Yet you mustn't forget one fact, Hi."

"What is that?"

"You mustn't forget that our fellows have already got their winning gait on this season."

"Humph! We'll see."

"It won't take us long, either," Dick continued. "There, the fellows are piling on the raft."

From the distance the spectators could see the two swimming teams lining up on the raft. They could also make out that Len Spencer was addressing the boys from the raft.

Bang! It was the warning shot. Spectators along the Gridley shore crowded close to the bank to get a better view.

Bang! At the second shot fourteen boys dived into the water almost in the same second. Fourteen heads came up, one after another, and the young swimmers settled down to their work. A launch followed along on each side of the course, to pick up any who needed help.

"It was thoughtful of some one to provide launches for the Central swimmers," leered Martin.

"I hope neither launch will be needed for any of our fellows," Dick responded. "If either school has to have a fellow picked up, then of course that's the school which loses the race."

Hi didn't answer. Despite his confident brag, he was now very anxious over the outcome.

Along came the swimmers, all doing well, making a fine showing for a crowd of fourteen boys whose average age was only fourteen years.

From time to time spectators cheered favorite boys in either squad.

"Central wins!" yelled one enthusiast, as the swimmers neared the stakeboat off the pier.

"Don't you believe it," yelled another. "Wait for the finish."

There wasn't long to wait. As the swimmers came nearer it was seen that Dave Darrin was ahead of all the swimmers, though Tom Reade was pressing him hard. Behind Tom came Bill Rodgers, then Greg Holmes, next two more North Grammar boys. Dan was next, with Harry following. The three tailenders were North Grammar boys.

"Central Grammar wins handily," announced Len Spencer through a megaphone.

Hi Martin's face darkened. "Anyway, I'll have the satisfaction of showing Dick Prescott my heels all the way up the course," he grunted.

"Now, you two individual racers tumble aboard, and get ready for your work," warned Len, as the launch ran in alongside the pier.

"Wipe him up, Dick!"

"Don't show him any mercy, Hi!"

Various other comments wafted to the pair as they sat in the launch facing each other.

"Some of those people must think we can both win," laughed Dick good-humoredly.

"I'll soon show you that only one of us can win," retorted Hi almost savagely.

Arrived at the raft, Len Spencer spoke briefly:

"At the first shot of the pistol you two youngsters take up your positions, ready to dive. At the second shot, or as soon after as you wish, you may dive and begin the race. Either contestant who dives before the second shot is heard will be disqualified and then the race will go to the other contestant."

Dick waited, tingling with the desire to win, though he knew that Martin was a splendid swimmer for his age.

"Are you ready?" asked Len in a low voice. Both boys nodded.

Bang! Len fired a revolver into the air, calling the attention of all spectators. Dick and Hi stepped nimbly to the edge of the raft, poising with hands pointed.

Bang! The splash was simultaneous as the swimmers struck the water. Each swimmer made a shallow dive and came up. Hi at once dropped into an overhead stroke, Dick relying upon a side stroke.

For the first seventy-five yards, as nearly as the onlookers could judge, the boys swam nose and nose.

"I'll tire this fellow out with a good pace, and then take a better one," thought Hi Martin. "I'm going to make a finish that will stop Dick Prescott from bragging whenever he sees me around hereafter."

Dick still swam well, but gradually Martin stole ahead of him.

"Where's Prescott now?" jeered a dozen North Grammar boys.

"Centrals, send out a launch to tow your champ! Then maybe he'll make better time."

Hi swam steadily and rapidly until he had more than half covered the course. Then he ventured on a look behind him.

"Prescott won't catch up all day," grinned Hi to himself. "Oh, I'm glad I insisted on this individual race!"

Gradually, and, to those on shore it seemed painfully, Dick gained on the leader. Still, when the race was almost over, Hi was well in the lead.

"Hi Martin! Hi Hi Hi!" yelled the North Grammar boys, dancing and tossing their caps in their glee. "Prescott, where art thou? Say, what did you try to get into the race for?"

"Now, I'll show the folks a few things," Hi resolved, putting on the best spurts of speed that were in him. It was truly a fine performance for a Grammar School boy.

Yet, to the amazement of most of the onlookers, Dick also was doing some very speedy swimming now. A yard he gained on Martin, then another and another. When they were still fifty yards from the stakeboat Dick suddenly changed his stroke and surged ahead, distinctly in the lead.

"Confound the human steam launch!" gasped Hi, almost choking, as he saw the powerful strokes of the swimmer ahead. "He'll make me look like a fool if I don't haul up on him——and the distance left is so confoundedly short!"

Now it could be seen that Martin was exerting every ounce of energy and strength that he possessed. Yet still young Prescott gained.

Then Martin foolishly lost his head altogether.

"If I can't win I'll make it look like a fluke!" he gritted.

Just as Dick was nearing the stakeboat, Hi threw up one hand.

"I've got a cramp!" he shouted. "Help!"

To some on shore he appeared about to sink. Dick passed the stakeboat, then turned like a flash and swam back toward Hi.

"Prescott wins!" called Len Spencer.

A few more strokes brought Dick up to where Hi pretended to flounder.

"Keep quiet, Hi, and let me get a hold on you," Dick offered. "I'll have you at the pier in a jiffy."

"You get away from me," snarled Martin. "I don't want any of your kind of help."

With that Hi appeared to forget his recent complaint of "cramp," for he made a lusty plunge toward the pier and pulled himself up.

Then, an instant later, he must have remembered, for he assumed an expression of pain and limped.

"There's that mean cramp again," he muttered. "I'd have won by a good many yards if it hadn't been for that."

Some of the Central Grammar boys nearby were impolite enough to laugh incredulously.

"Oh, I've dropped my handbag into the river!" exclaimed one woman to another suddenly, at the end of the pier.

The other woman turned, giving a quick, startled glance toward the water.

"I—-I don't know how it happened," gasped the loser. "There it is, away down the stream, floating toward that boathouse. Oh, Master Prescott, do you feel able to go and get it for me?"

"I'll do it with pleasure, madam," Dick nodded. He looked for a moment. Then, seeing a black floating object, he started after it, his stroke apparently none the weaker after his swift race.

It had floated nearly under the boathouse at the water end. The building in question belonged to the estate next to that from which the swimming contests had been conducted. This boathouse was closed, for the owners had not yet come to Gridley for the summer. The windows of the little green building were shuttered from the inside. Over the water the walls came down to within six inches of the present level of water.

Keeping his eyes turned toward the black, floating object, Dick swam easily to the spot. The black object floated under the open sidewall into the boathouse. Just as Dick got there he dived, duck fashion, head first, and passed to the interior of the boathouse at the river end.

As he came up inside Dick's first discovery was that of artificial light in the boathouse. Then his gaze rested on the platform end over the land.

"Amos Garwood here, of all places!" gasped the astonished Grammar School boy.

Chapter XXIV

CONCLUSION

The mentally queer inventor had rigged up a bench just under shelves on which rested tools and boat supplies.

Just at the moment the inventor had his back turned to the water as he stood working at his bench. Dick was able to look at him while not in immediate danger of being seen himself.

How quietly the Grammar School boy trod water! He hardly dared breathe, for fear of giving an alarm.

Yet, even in all his astonishment, Prescott did not forget to let one hand close over the handle of the black bag whose recovery had brought him here.

"I can't do anything with Garwood alone," reflected Dick swiftly. "I must get out, if I can, without making a noise, and then give the hurry alarm. That fellow is mixing something, and, if he isn't stopped soon, he's quite likely to blow up the boathouse, himself included."

Fortunately there was sufficient depth of water at this outer end of the boathouse. Prescott let himself sink so quietly that there was barely a ripple above his head. Next, with a few cautious strokes, he carried himself past the hanging side wall and into the open upstream.

"Gracious, but no wonder Garwood has been able to keep away from pursuers," thought the boy excitedly, as he swam steadily up toward the other pier. "He has a place where not even a Sherlock Holmes would ever think of looking for him. Why, he could work, sleep and eat there and never give a sign of his presence!"

"Did you get it?" called the owner of the handbag eagerly.

"Yes, ma'am," Dick replied.

"The bag wasn't open, was it?"

"No, ma'am."

"Let me have it quickly, please. Oh, I'm so thankful! Here is my purse with all the money safe and sound. Wait, Master Prescott, I must reward you suitably."

"No; I thank you," Dick replied, his color rising. "Your thanks are enough. I've been taught that courtesy can't be repaid with cash. You are very, very welcome to any service that I was able to do you."

As Dick hurried into the Central Grammar "dressing room" he found all five of his chums waiting to rub him down and help him dress.

"Here, give me that towel, and get out on other business in a hurry!" begged Dick. "Dave! Tom! Amos Garwood is in the boathouse below here, working at a bench. Get some of the men and rush down there to make a capture. Greg, run and see to it that a launch moves down to the river end of the boathouse in case Garwood tries to get out that way when he hears the alarm!"

Prescott's chums darted out in a hurry. Dick half dried himself in a few frenzied dabs with the towel. Then he pulled on his clothing faster than ever before.

He got outside on the pier just in time to see Dave and Tom leading a dozen men stealthily toward the door of the boathouse. Out on the water Len Spencer's launch, with half a dozen men in it, stood as river sentinel.

While those approaching the boathouse door were still more than a score of feet away there came a startling interruption.

Bang! sounded inside. The door of the building strained an instant, but did not give way.

"That's our old friend, Amos bang-bang, to a dot," muttered Tom dryly, as the advancing party of men and boys halted.

"I don't care about fooling with a dynamite factory," remarked one of the men.

Dick, at a dead run, joined the party.

"Come along!" he cried. "Let's break down the door and find out whether the poor fellow is hurt."

"Yes! And have that 'poor fellow' hand you a peck of nitro-glycerine for a surprise," retorted a man.

"Come on, fellows! We can get the door down without help," Dick called, appealing to his chums.

All five of them rallied to his support. It took but a few sturdy shoulder blows to complete the work of the explosion and break the lock of the door.

Dick took one quick look inside.

"Tom, run and 'phone for a physician!" Prescott called back. "Poor Garwood is unconscious, and cut. He's bleeding. Poor chap, with his lop-sided mind and his 'mastery of the world' imaginings!"

Reade sped away. As soon as the crowd found there was no danger there was a rush to the scene. Darrin and three friends managed to hold the crowd somewhat at bay, while Prescott assisted two women in trying to bring the injured man to.

"I hope he doesn't get away this time," thought Dick. "If Garwood remains at large much longer he'll fix up a bang-bang that will carry him clean into the next world!"

While those having the injured man in charge waited they explored the boathouse. Of the explosive materials not a particle was found. Evidently it had all gone up in smoke. But, in a far corner, the searchers discovered a package of gauze, and another of salve, with which poor Garwood had evidently attended to the burns resulting from former explosions. Later it was found that both packages came from a drugstore some twenty miles away, where the poor fellow had also bought his explosive materials from time to time. He must have walked the long distance at night when other people were abed, for the druggist stated that his customer came in, on each visit, as soon as the store was opened in the morning.

Blankets and a few groceries, found in the loft, explained the demented man's manner of housekeeping during the last few days.

It was half an hour ere a physician finally arrived in a touring car.

"The man doesn't appear to be badly hurt," declared the medical man. "It won't take us five minutes to get him into town and in the hospital, so I believe we had better start to revive him after we get him there."

Two strong men were found who were willing to sit in the tonneau, holding Amos Garwood's insensible body between them.

As the car started away a subdued cheer arose. The mystery and the vanishing of Amos Garwood were at an end at last. Those who had feared having a demented man at large in the community breathed more easily.

From the day of the race the summer vacation for the late Grammar School boys began in earnest. A few days later Dick and his swimming squad met a similar organization from the South Grammar, and a match was held on the river. As Prescott's squad again won, Central Grammar was now undisputed Grammar School champion on the water as well as in baseball.

Colonel Garwood tried to pay the offered reward to the members of Dick & Co., but the parents of the boys refused to entertain the idea.

Amos Garwood, not seriously injured in body, was soon well enough to be taken back to the sanitarium. Here his malady was found not to be severe. A year later he was discharged, fully cured of his delusions, and able once more to take his place as a useful member of society.

There does not remain a great deal more to be told.

Many of the boys who have appeared in these pages went no further in school life, but stepped out into the working world, there to fit themselves for the men's places in life.

The more fortunate ones, however, went to High School. All the members of Dick & Co. were thus favored in being able to go forward into the fields of higher education. We shall speedily meet with these manly American boys again, for their further doings will be described in the *High School Boys' Series*.

In the first volume of this series, "*The High School Freshmen; Or Dick & Co.'s First Year Pranks and Sports*," the friends of these six wide-awake boys will find them in a new field of action, and follow them through an exciting series of trials and triumphs. Dick & Co.'s interest in High School athletics, and the way in which they won a permanent place in the hearts of the older students is told so realistically in the first volume of this series as to make all readers long to know more about them.

All the big and little boys who wish to continue their friendship with Dick & Co. will find their further adventures related most entertainingly in the four volumes of the High School Boys' Series just published.